The Dreamweavers

G. Z. SCHMIDT

HOLIDAY HOUSE · New York

Library of Congress Cataloging-in-Publication Data

Names: Schmidt, G. Z. (Gail Zhuang), author.

Title: The dreamweavers / G. Z. Schmidt.

Description: First edition. | New York : Holiday House, [2021] |
Audience: Ages 8-12. | Audience: Grades 4-6. | Summary: "Twin
siblings journey through the City of Ashes and visit the Jade Rabbit to
save their grandpa in this Chinese folklore-inspired fantasy
adventure"—Provided by publisher.

Identifiers: LCCN 2021002191 (print) | LCCN 2021002192 (ebook) |
ISBN 9780823444236 (hardcover) | ISBN 9780823450251 (ebook)

Subjects: CYAC: Folklore—China—Fiction. | Kings, queens, rulers,
etc.—Fiction. | Brothers and sisters—Fiction. | Twins—Fiction.
China—History—Ming dynasty, 1368-1644—Fiction.

Classification: LCC PZ7.1.S33618 Dr 2021 (print) | LCC PZ7.1.S33618
(ebook) | DDC [Fic]—dc23

LC record available at https://lccn.loc.gov/2021002191

LC ebook record available at https://lccn.loc.gov/2021002192

ISBN: 978-0-8234-4423-6 (hardcover)

For Grandma

CONTENTS

CHAPTER ONE

—

The Dreamweaver

*M*any moons ago, there was a small village in the mountains of southern China. During the day, the village was like any other scattered across the country. But sometimes at night, just past bedtime, a remarkable thing would happen there.

It would happen after the firewood cooled beneath kitchen stoves, after oil lamps winked out behind windows, one by one; after conversations in each house dwindled to drowsy whispers and a breath of quiet swept across the sleepy village. It was a time when even the rowdiest children gave up their struggle to stay awake.

In the sky above, soft clouds would nestle the bright moon as its white light smeared the glassy waters of the Pearl River nearby, where schools of colorful fish slept beneath the smooth surface.

None of the villagers would be awake by the time a mysterious figure emerged on one of the drifting clouds.

But if any of them happened to sit up and glance outside, they'd see the hunched figure carried what looked like a fishing rod.

Yet this was no ordinary fisherman.

The man would sit cross-legged on the edge of the cloud, his silhouette illuminated by the bloated moon behind him. He'd dangle the rod in the air and then cast a line, as easily as if he were fishing from a rowboat on the river.

For the next few hours, he'd quietly reel in his invisible catches and place them carefully into a porcelain jar.

Then, as silently as he had appeared, he'd vanish into the shadows.

None of the villagers ever laid eyes on him, or on the mysterious things that he placed in his jar.

But I have, from my quiet home on the moon above.

And I've seen two children with him on those clouds. One boy and one girl.

CHAPTER TWO

—

The Duel

Ming Dynasty, 1500s A.D.

Mei pointed her weapon upward like an umbrella. With her strong pose and steady concentration, the twelve-year-old could almost pass as a warrior from the Imperial City—that is, if the warriors wore tunics, used knobby branches as swords, and were forced to wait an eternity for their dueling partners to present themselves.

"Hurry up, Yun," she sighed.

"Wait," replied Mei's twin brother, who approached slowly, holding a similar wooden branch. He fumbled with the stick, trying to find the best way to grip it between his fingers. "There's a proper way to hold this in combat, in order to maximize the length of the blade. Well, the *imaginary* blade," Yun corrected himself matter-of-factly. "This, of course, is merely a substitute for a real sword—"

"Come *on!* I've *been* waiting for five minutes."

"All right, all right."

Yun took his place so that the pair stood opposite each other in the shade of a willow tree beside the Pearl River. They were identical in terms of age and most features—dark eyes, straight black hair, lightly toasted skin—but their personalities were as different as night and day. Mei was the impatient one—adults often said she was as restless as an ant on a frying pan. Yun was the careful, cautious one who adults said moved at an ant's pace.

Above the willow tree, the sky was a pale blue, the morning sun unusually warm. The calendar said late autumn, but the air felt like early summer. The yellowing grass tickled the twins' bare feet. The siblings, however, didn't have time to appreciate the weather. More important things were at stake that morning. They'd made a bet earlier that whoever lost the duel had to give the winner their share of desserts for a week. As the Mid-Autumn Festival was two days away, a loss meant missing out on their grandpa's famous batch of mooncakes.

And that was out of the question.

"All right, on the count of three." Mei readied her stance. "One..."

"...two..." counted Yun.

"Three!"

They swung their sticks. Wood bounced off wood. Mei separated easily and jumped forward, her black braids swaying. Her branch sliced the air and hit Yun's knee. With a yelp, Yun tumbled backward.

"Well, that was easy," said Mei.

"That's not fair," protested Yun, rubbing his backside. "You know I'm nearsighted."

Like most of the other villagers, Mei and Yun's family were too poor to afford eyeglasses. Yun had grown accustomed to navigating with blurry vision, and most of the time it wasn't a big deal. But certain endeavors, like dueling, avoiding mud puddles, or counting approaching horses, proved tricky.

Mei rolled her eyes. "We were standing inches apart, not miles!" She also noted it was odd that Yun claimed to be blind as a bat, yet was sharper than an owl whenever the bedsheets at home weren't perfectly symmetrical, or when Mei's dish had two more bean sprouts than Yun's.

"That's different," replied Yun, who prided himself on his precision and neatness. "It's much easier to see what stands out when it shouldn't. Anyway, let's start over. This time, we'll give me a three-second head start."

"Why?"

"The extra three seconds make up for my lack of good eyesight, and subsequent reaction time. It's only fair. No, wait. Actually, four seconds is better."

"*Four*? You'd have me beaten in four!"

After several more minutes of arguing, the twins decided to call a temporary truce until they figured out a new way of determining a winner. Yun lay down in the shade, thinking, while Mei began climbing the willow tree.

Mei was a good climber—the best in their village. She had a lightweight build and was quick on her feet. She could tell which branches were the sturdiest and identify invisible grooves for footholds. By the time Yun looked up, his sister was already high above the ground.

From the tree's canopy, Mei could see past the village. The Pearl River snaked around a bend and continued into the surrounding hills and mountains. The nearest place, the City of Ashes, was a day's journey away by foot.

Nobody in their right mind would go there. It was rumored to be a dreadful area, full of burnt buildings and empty houses. Haunted, too. Strange happenings had been reported by those who had passed the city's outskirts: accounts of footprints appearing where no one had walked, and the sound of crowds sobbing where there wasn't a single soul in sight. Travelers told of a gray fog that weighed down the city, casting the place in an eternal cloud of woe.

When Mei and Yun were toddlers, Grandpa used to tell the children stories about what he knew of the City of Ashes in its olden days. He'd describe in his hushed voice the city's once-magnificent buildings, how the sloped rooftops had been gilded with intricate designs, how the trees there would blossom into brilliant shades of pink in the spring. Grandpa used to tell these stories, back before Mei and Yun came to realize that their parents had disappeared behind the city's walls. After that, it became a sore subject.

Mei climbed back down the tree and plopped next to her brother. They observed a fat beetle in the grass for a few moments; the bug appeared to be sleeping in a wisp of a bright blue cloud.

"Let's go check on Grandpa," suggested Mei, who grew bored quickly. "He probably has the first batch of mooncakes ready. We might as well eat while we think of a new contest."

They went back up to the village, which thrummed with life as the new day got underway. Farmers headed toward the fields with baskets balanced on their shoulders. Young adults bearing axes headed toward the mountains, from where they'd later return with freshly chopped firewood. Toddlers played with sticks and rag dolls on porches. Mei and Yun raced down the dirt road, greeting each villager by name. Everyone knew one another in the small community.

"Hi Mao-Mao! Hi Po! Good morning, Madam Hu—sorry, we have to go, Grandpa is expecting us!" they added before the nosy woman could trap them in one of her hour-long gossip sessions.

They hurried toward their small wooden house at the end of the lane. A familiar, sweet smell drifted out the open kitchen window. As the twins burst through the door, they saw their grandpa taking out a steaming hot pan from the stove. When he saw the two children, he grinned.

"Impeccable timing," he remarked.

The mooncakes gleamed. Each one had a beautiful, swirling pattern etched on the crusty top. The twins' mouths watered at the sight of the little golden pastries. Beneath the kitchen table, their fat gray cat, Smelly Tail, yowled hopefully. When Mei and Yun were four, their mother had brought Smelly Tail home from the fields, where she'd rescued the cat from a pack of angry dogs. The cat had distrusted the family at first, hissing at anyone who came close, but she hung around for Grandpa's cooking. She'd been living in their kitchen for the last eight years, better fed than any other cat.

It didn't surprise the family that Smelly Tail stayed. Grandpa was the best cook in the village. It was said that anything and everything turned to magic on Grandpa's earthen stove. Fishermen often dropped by with a bucket of freshly caught carp for the family in exchange for a piping-hot bowl of Grandpa's soup. Same with farmers, who came to the door with extra baskets of vegetables and left with steaming plates of fried rice.

But Grandpa's mooncakes were the best of all. Every month on the full moon, he created a batch of mooncakes for the whole village to share. They were made from his secret recipe that not even Mei and Yun knew. Sometimes the cake filling would taste sweet, like honey. Other times it had the crisp, toasty taste of sesame. Whatever the filling, whenever anyone ate one, their day would visibly brighten. Whether someone was sad about the loss of a pet, or frustrated with a neighbor, or worried about the crops, every little problem seemed to vanish after eating Grandpa's mooncakes. Grandpa claimed it was due to a special ingredient, which he never revealed.

The twins plopped down at the rickety wooden table to the side of the hearth. The kitchen wasn't large. Grandpa's clay bowls and utensils cluttered what little space there was. Connected by a narrow entryway was the rest of the house— one bedroom for Grandpa, one bedroom for Mei and Yun to share, a small washroom, and the room that the twins' parents had once occupied. This last room was now empty save for piles of old scrolls and forgotten belongings.

"You two had breakfast less than an hour ago," said Grandpa, wiping flour from his gray hair. "I'm starting to feed you as much as I feed Smelly Tail here. Yet you both are still as skinny as a pair of willow rods."

"Dueling is hard work," answered Yun.

"Yes, all three seconds of it," chimed in Mei with a slight eye roll.

Grandpa chuckled lightly. "Well, I'm afraid these mooncakes have to sit for two nights before they're fully ready. Right now they're all flaky." His eyes swept over the twins' eager faces. "But I suppose you can have a taste."

He took a pair of chopsticks and carefully cut off a small chunk from one of the crumbly cakes. The inside oozed black sesame paste. Grandpa made a *wait* motion with his finger. He carefully put the piece of mooncake into his mouth and closed his eyes.

"Not bad," he said after a moment. "Of course, I haven't added the secret ingredient yet. Saving that for the final batch. But I trust they will impress the emperor's son."

"The emperor's son?" repeated Mei and Yun.

Grandpa nodded. It was clear he was trying to act nonchalant, but his crinkled smile gave him away. He pulled up the last chair and sat beside the twins. "Yes, it seems word of my mooncakes has reached the Imperial City. Several envoys arrived a month ago to let me know the emperor's favorite son is attending our Mid-Autumn celebration to personally sample them."

Mei and Yun exchanged a startled glance. This was huge news. Their small village was one of those insignificant places that mapmakers could barely trace, and rarely got visits from high government officials.

"And you kept this a secret from us the whole time?" exclaimed Mei.

"I don't remember the envoys," added Yun.

"They came by one morning when you were in the orchards—spending more time eating plums than picking them, I might add," said Grandpa with a grin. "The whole village knows."

"What if the emperor's son likes your mooncakes so much that he asks you to work as the emperor's personal cook?" asked Mei excitedly. "At the palace headquarters?"

"The Imperial City," murmured Yun, chewing his fingernails—a habit he did whenever he was nervous or excited, or both. The twins had heard many fantastical stories about the Imperial City, where all the high officials and the emperor lived. Their father, who had been a scholar before his disappearance, had briefly lived there in his younger days. He was the only person in their village who had done so.

"Baba once told me the palace has tens of *thousands* of valuable scrolls," Yun said dreamily.

"And plenty of people I could *properly* duel, I bet," said Mei. "You'd move there if they asked you, right, Grandpa?" she added.

Grandpa chuckled again. "That's a lofty goal for some, but not for me. I have no intention of moving from my village, my home."

No one really knew how long Grandpa had lived in the village. He claimed to have been there when the village had only three houses and the surrounding trees had been mere saplings. He was certainly old (though not as old as their neighbor Elder Liu, whose skin was so wrinkly it resembled a prune). Whenever Mei or Yun tried to guess Grandpa's real age, he'd smile and say he was "just old enough to keep going."

Grandpa carefully cut two more chunks off the mooncake for Mei and Yun. "Eat up, and once you're done, Madam Hu told me she needs help preparing the festival lanterns," he said. As the twins groaned in unison, he reminded them gently, "It's important we all play a part in the community."

Each year, the Mid-Autumn Festival caused a great stir of excitement among the villagers. Families would cook large meals from the season's harvest, and Farmer Jao would roast his fattest pig for the occasion. It was a time of gratitude. The entire village would celebrate together under the moon and stars, laughing and eating and dancing to music, until they finished off the night with Grandpa's famous mooncakes. The moon that night was always the brightest and roundest of the year.

Mei and Yun went outside. There were even more people milling about than before, preparing for the festival. The village had already started to put up decorations two days in advance. A group of small children were carrying baskets of chrysanthemum petals they'd gathered from the riverbed. Several teenage boys lugged wooden pillars to the entrance to hold the golden banners.

They saw Yun and sneered, as they usually did, "Get lost, runt. This isn't a task for wimpy, fog-brained scholar boys."

Yun felt his face heat up. Before he could say anything, Mei tugged him along. She didn't want her brother to launch another one of his embarrassing, longwinded retorts that never worked to stop the bullies, who would also turn on her soon enough if they didn't get moving. "Ignore them," she whispered, throwing the teenagers a dirty look. "They're just insecure. Come on, let's go find Madam Hu."

Despite the closeness of the small village, the twins were not popular with the other kids. There were several reasons for this, as you'll soon discover. Luckily, it never bothered Mei and Yun *too* much, because for them, having a twin was like having a best friend day and night. (It was also a little like having a shadow, in the times they annoyed each other.)

Madam Hu was on her porch, supervising the paper lantern distribution. Her lips were stained crimson above her sharp chin. Mei and Yun liked to joke that the color came from the blood of those who dared to cross her. Which was nearly everyone in the village, at some point or another.

"There you are," she snapped at the approaching twins. "Hurry, hurry. We haven't got all day. Grab a lantern, both of you, and start filling them. Candles are over there."

Each paper lantern was the size of a winter squash. Madam Hu and the other women in the village had been working on them for two months, crafting them out of a bamboo frame and bright gauze dyed red for good luck. The insides had a hollow center for holding one small candle, which the twins helped fill. On the night of the festival, the lanterns would be released into the sky like floating pieces of sunlight.

While they worked, Madam Hu gossiped as per her usual habit. After a ten-minute tirade about her lazy neighbor, Madam Lee, who left laundry out to dry for days on end, she changed tacks to the subject of Grandpa. Was it true, she demanded of the twins, that the emperor's son was coming all the way from the Imperial City, just for Grandpa's special mooncakes? And wasn't it an absolute disgrace that the officials had not heard of *her* renowned soup dumplings?

"Grandpa's mooncakes will be the talk of the nation," replied Mei proudly.

"*Hmph*," snorted Madam Hu, pinching a lantern with her long fingers. "That old fool thinks too highly of himself. Your whole family did. Teaching you two to read, for instance, and so young. What nonsense."

Even though their small village did not have a school, the

twins' parents had often stressed the importance of knowing how to read and write. After their parents' disappearance, Grandpa taught the twins at home from scrolls and other materials belonging to their father. They also learned arithmetic and how to use an abacus (which, as far as the twins could tell, was only useful for keeping track of points for card games).

"What good are book smarts in a place out here?" Madam Hu continued. "You only need good looks if you're a woman out to get a good husband, and strong muscles if you're a man out to get a good wife. Anything else is ambition. Ambition only leads to downfall. Look at what happened to your—" She suddenly squawked like a surprised hen, and yelled at Yun for creasing one of the paper lanterns. The twins spent the rest of the afternoon being lectured on how to properly handle the gauze.

That night before bed, Mei chided Yun for creasing the lantern on purpose.

Yun didn't say anything. A thought came to him. "If Grandpa does manage to gain favor with the emperor's son," he said, "do you think we could...?" But then he fell silent again and began brushing his fingers along the chipped windowsill.

"What?" asked Mei as she adjusted the bamboo pillow on her bed.

"Nothing. I'm just mad about what Madam Hu said earlier." In response to Mei's raised eyebrow, Yun sighed and lowered his voice. "I was thinking, the emperor has a lot of power and resources. Maybe the palace has an investigator who can find out what happened to..."

He didn't finish the sentence. He didn't need to.

"Why would anyone from the palace help us?" replied Mei, suddenly irritated. "We're nobody. Besides, we don't need their help. We know where Mama and Baba are."

"Sure." Now Yun sounded irritated, too. He was too tired to remind her that they only knew where Mama and Baba *went*.

"They're fine," Mei said, as if reading Yun's mind. "We'll find them on our own one day. Grandpa won't be able to stop us forever."

Both siblings lay on their beds without another word. They stared out the window. The moon hung in the evening sky. It was nearly a perfect circle, its surface a lovely blend of gold and white, the light pressing against the shadows. But the sight only made Mei and Yun feel worse.

Because there had been a full moon, just like this one, when their parents had disappeared six years ago.

CHAPTER THREE

≡

The City of Blossoms

*T*he City of Ashes had not always been called by such a *dreary name. Once upon a time, it had been known as the City of Blossoms. In the springtime, beautiful trees bloomed pink along the city's green pastures—cherry blossoms and peach blossoms, their millions of petals dancing in the sunlight. Artists and poets from all over the country traveled to the city in order to capture its splendor on paper.*

One year, an exceptionally talented poet arrived from the Imperial City, seeking a change of scenery and new inspiration. People nicknamed the young woman Lotus because she was as lovely as the flower. She was witty and good-natured, and she had long, gleaming black hair, which she often twirled absentmindedly around her ink brush as she worked on her poems. As pleasant as Lotus was, her words were even more enchanting. She had an ingenious way of using descriptions and metaphors. She could make a tiny ant seem as if it were king of the animals. She could extinguish the sun's brilliance and cloak it with the darkness of night.

As the months went by, the thriving city continued to grow and attract more people, including scholars, aristocrats, and the like. One particular nobleman arrived. He was called the Noble General.

Everyone in the city soon knew about the Noble General, though it quickly became clear that the title was used rather ironically by everyone but himself. He bragged constantly about his ties to the emperor. He liked to make fun of the artists' paintings, though he himself could only draw stick figures. He scorned the writers who read from their works, though the only writing he excelled at was tax decrees. He trampled the flowers on his path with indifference.

As soon as he met Lotus, he was set on making her his wife.

"I've turned down many great women, but you seem worthy enough," he told Lotus one morning.

"That is kind of you," Lotus replied shortly.

"Then it's settled. We'll depart tomorrow for the Imperial City. I'll ask the palace to host a grand feast this Friday for the wedding, where you will dress in your finest gown. Obviously, you'll have to stop writing your silly poetry once we're married. That's no job for a proper woman. You will bear me ten sons, and—"

"Excuse me, but I never agreed to marry you," said Lotus.

She had heard about the Noble General's notorious behavior. Unbeknownst to him, she'd written several poems about him that made all the children in the city giggle, including one titled "He Walks and Talks Like a Baboon."

"You—you won't marry me?" the Noble General sputtered. "Why not?"

In fact, many men had asked Lotus for her hand in marriage, and she was used to politely turning them down. She explained calmly how she was already in love with someone else.

"Who?" the nobleman demanded.

"I'm in love with the man who plants and cares for the trees and flowers," answered Lotus. "He makes miracles grow from the soil. He breathes life into everything he touches. My heart blooms in his hands."

And indeed, while Lotus wrote about the blossoms, the city gardener planted them. Lotus and Gardener Wong were often seen talking and laughing together along the city's paths. As the gardener tended the flowers and trees, Lotus would whisper to them—uplifting words like "grow," "flourish," and "shine." Her words seemed to have an extraordinary effect on the plants, so that those she spoke to always seemed greener and larger, their petals glistening with more shades of pink than others. They caught your eye the same way the brightest stars in the sky do.

After a tender courtship, Lotus and the city gardener announced their marriage. The entire city celebrated with fireworks and helped plant new rows of bright, dazzling flowers along the city perimeter. A year later, the couple had a beautiful baby son.

But the Noble General never forgot his rejection. He couldn't believe that he'd been passed over for a lowly, uneducated gardener.

"Nobody makes a fool of me," he snarled. "They will pay. They will all pay. Mark my words."

CHAPTER FOUR

四

A Notable Festival

When the twins awoke the next day, the weather had changed notably. A set of heavy, lifeless clouds blanketed the village. They loomed so close that grayish white wisps touched the rooftops. There was something particularly dismal about these clouds, so that everything underneath them felt extra cold and extra dreary.

Mei and Yun felt extra sullen from the sudden gloom. They argued over their bowls of porridge at breakfast. Yun accidentally stepped on Smelly Tail's tail, causing the already cranky cat to scratch everything in its reach, which caused Mei to drop and break three plates.

After Mei had cleaned the mess and tended to her clawed ankles, the twins went outside. They realized quickly that no one else in the village was having a good day, either. People bickered left and right over the smallest things. Kai, the one child in the village who never made fun of the twins, refused to play with them. Around noon, Mao-Mao's father, who normally was the calmest man in the village, nearly got in a fistfight with Farmer Jao. Miss Bing dropped a basket of sweet potatoes and caused a thirty-minute screaming session among five people claiming she was trying to trip them. In the afternoon, Doctor Po stormed out of his house, smashed an egg on his porch, and shouted, "I give up! Why prescribe medicine if no one listens?"

"Everyone's acting as if they ate coals for breakfast," observed Yun.

"It's strange," agreed Mei.

Grandpa also noted the villagers' unusual behavior. "This whole affair with the emperor's son must have brought on unexpected stress for the whole community," he guessed. "People tend to lose their heads in the face of royalty."

"Hopefully the moon is visible tomorrow evening," said Mei. "In time for the festival."

"Not to worry," said Grandpa with a smile. "My moon-cakes shall make everyone happy again, whether or not the sky cooperates."

Grandpa was optimistic like that. In spite of life's hardships, he rarely worried about things. When he'd broken his wrist a few years ago after climbing a tree to rescue Smelly Tail, all he did was smile and say, "Now I get to enjoy tea with Doctor Po."

It was Grandpa who kept reassuring Mei and Yun that their parents were well, that they were simply busy learning all they could about the City of Ashes. *Research was hard work*, he'd told them. *Don't be angry with them for being gone.*

Three months stretched to six, then twelve. But not to worry, their parents would return for the twins' seventh birthday. Three missed birthdays later, when the twins finally began trying to sneak to the city themselves, Grandpa had stopped them and repeated gently but firmly, "Be patient. Sometimes life takes us in unexpected directions."

✷

The clouds did not disappear overnight. On the morning of the festival, they loomed even closer, a wall of gray. Around midday, they started rolling oddly, as if a breeze had sent them rippling across the sky, like when a stone is dropped in water.

Except there was no wind to move them. The villagers had never seen such a thing.

"It's a bad omen," Elder Liu warned the villagers. "These clouds are a sign of ancient magic." Elder Liu tended to ramble about things like that, reading too much into tea leaves and discarded chicken bones.

Weird weather or none, the festivities had to go on.

Mei and Yun put an extra effort into their appearance. They washed their faces and braided their hair. Mei had dug out her mother's special butterfly hairpin and placed it in her braid.

They ate their breakfast anxiously. Grandpa was the only one at the table who seemed untroubled. After breakfast, Grandpa began making spiced fish stew for the festival and sent Mei and Yun to help the other villagers with the final preparations.

Everyone had put on their best clothes and looked clean and polished. Even Dandan, a five-year-old who played in the mud as much as the pigs did, had been scrubbed clean by his mother from head to toe. (When Mei and Yun saw him, they thought he ironically resembled a pig even more, as his newly washed skin was raw pink.)

Spotless as the villagers looked, there was still no change in their attitudes. Nobody spoke to one another. Children sat off by themselves instead of playing together. Families glared at one another, as if daring the others to make the first wrong move. There were no greetings, no laughter or friendly smiles. Madam Hu, who wore an overly flowery robe, stood menacingly on her porch. She was in a fouler mood than the twins had ever seen her, ready to bark at anyone who passed. Mei and Yun decided it was best to lie low until the festivities started, rather than help with the final preparations and risk angering anyone further.

They retreated to a private spot near their favorite willow tree by the river. From the bank, they dangled branches and tried to make ripple patterns in the water, one of their favorite pastimes, but it turned out to be difficult that day. The normally calm river was as turbulent as the clouds above. So they gave up and instead sat back and watched the misty yellow-and-blue fog that had started rolling over the grass.

That was the main reason the twins were unpopular with the other children in the village. Mei and Yun often saw things that the others didn't: soft mists hovering over the river of fish, or sunny wisps of smoke hanging above Smelly Tail's ears as the cat slept. They knew their parents had seen them, too, or at least their mother did. Mama had often pointed out the colored clouds the way one might describe the weather, with casual remarks like, "The grasses are looking light blue today," or, "Poor Farmer Jao always sleeps in a haze of purple."

When the twins were younger, the appearance of such colors and vapors seemed perfectly ordinary. It was a part of their everyday lives; they did not fear it, nor did they question it, the same way you might not normally question why everyone needs sleep or why people laugh when they're happy. But it quickly became apparent that this ability, whatever it was, was not normal. The other kids in the village simply did not see random, colorful clouds in a room, did not see little wafts of blue or yellow fog lingering above a toddler or a field of grasshoppers. Mei had once asked Grandpa about it, but he'd just said it was perfectly fine and not to worry—though that was easy for Grandpa to say because *he* wasn't the one being called "fog-brained" by the other children in the village. Afterward, the twins began keeping their observations to themselves.

Madam Lilian and her husband, Mister Ahn, passed by on their daily walk.

Normally, Madam Lilian would affectionately pinch the twins' cheeks and offer them candied fruits. But today, she shot them a frosty look and clucked, "Lazy, ungrateful orphans, whiling away the hours by the river while their grandfather is toiling in the kitchen. Children like that never show their appreciation for adults."

"If anything, you should blame their parents," her husband replied, in the way grown-ups sometimes talk as if children don't have ears.

The story of the twins' parents was no secret in the village. It wasn't just Madam Hu who had an opinion of their parents' ambitions and interests. Mei and Yun often overheard the other villagers' whispers about their family behind their backs. *How unfortunate it is for Old Wu, who must bear the burden of feeding two extra mouths after the parents dis-appeared*, some said. *Poor, foolish scholars*, their parents had been called. *Always had grand notions of gaining infinite knowledge about the outside world instead of tending the fields and family*, murmur murmur. But the villagers didn't actually know what had happened to Mei and Yun's parents. Nobody did. All anyone knew was that they'd ventured into the City of Ashes six years ago for research purposes, promising to return within three months, and had never been seen again.

Yun glared at the retreating backs of Madam Lilian and Mister Ahn, then turned to his sister. "I still think this is our chance," he said in a low voice. "The emperor's son coming to our village is a once-in-a-lifetime opportunity."

"No, not this investigator stuff again," groaned Mei.

"It doesn't hurt to ask! If anything, we can just ask him if the rumors about the City of Ashes are true. The emperor's son is bound to know what goes on across China. If the city is as strange and dangerous as people say, he can confirm"—Yun's voice caught in the back of his throat—"confirm the questions we have," he finished.

Mei threw a pebble into the water. Her brother could be quite stubborn, like a bruise that wouldn't fade. "Don't ask on the day of the Mid-Autumn Festival," she said.

"Why not?" challenged Yun, who thought his sister was equally stubborn.

Mei shook out her hair to readjust the butterfly pin. She held the hairpin in her hands for a moment. Their mother once said it had been carved from a magical bamboo tree in the mountains. It was supposed to draw out the natural beauty in every girl who wore it. Mei had worn it the last few years for special occasions, and Madam Hu or another adult would chortle, *Looks like the magic didn't work this time. Perhaps you played in the dirt too much.* It was likely they thought the hairpin's purported magic was Mama's way of encouraging Mei to be more like those good, graceful girls in the village—the kind of girls who didn't climb trees or play in the dirt or do cartwheels. What they did not know was that Mama never minded those things, and she always told Mei she was lovely whether she wore the hairpin or not.

"Why *not*?" Yun said again, jarring Mei from her memory.

"Because the Mid-Autumn Festival is a time of happiness," answered Mei, tracing the bronze butterfly with her finger. "Not a time of dwelling on the bad."

"Yes, *happiness*," repeated Yun wryly. "Because everyone in the village is so happy right now." Suddenly, an idea came to him—one that he was sure would appeal to his sister's competitive nature. "I just thought of something to replace our bet from the other day."

Mei put the pin back in her braid and looked at him with interest. "What is it?"

"Only this time, we won't be wagering on dessert," said Yun. "I'm thinking of a bet with much higher stakes."

"I'm listening."

"Since everyone's in such a bad mood, I bet you the emperor's son won't smile at all tonight. If I'm right, we talk to him about the City of Ashes."

"That's a terrible wager," scoffed Mei. "He will too smile. It's the Mid-Autumn Festival!"

"Fine, if you think his joy is so certain, then how about this? If the emperor's son smiles at least *seven* times tonight,

I'll drop the subject. We won't tell him about Mama and Baba or ask about the city. But if he doesn't..." Yun let the prospect of approaching the powerful prince hang in the air.

Mei thought again about the past day and the gloom that hung over everyone in the village. "Seven times?"

"Or more."

Mei sucked in her breath. She'd rather make bets about things she could control, like tree-climbing or dueling. A whole other person's mood was something else. As fearless as Mei tried to be, the idea of approaching a royal prince for help in the event that she lost the wager did not appeal to her. Then again, it was the Mid-Autumn Festival. How could she lose? And, as most people with a twin or sibling would agree, proving her brother wrong was something she couldn't resist.

"Fine. Deal."

✳

Evening arrived quickly. The villagers gathered outside under the cloudy night sky, murmuring and waiting for the arrival of the emperor's son. The golden moon, which managed to peek in every now and then from behind the rolling clouds, was a perfect circle. Red-and-gold streamers, lanterns, and banners glimmered at the village entrance where the people stood. The scene looked perfect, if not for the fact there wasn't a single smile in the crowd.

Grandpa accompanied Mei and Yun to the gathering. He whistled cheerfully along the dirt road as he carried his special dish of mooncakes under one arm.

"They'll be great, Grandpa," Yun reassured him. He bit into his barely visible thumbnail, which he'd nervously gnawed over the past few nights. "You're the greatest chef in the village. There's no reason why the emperor's son will hate your mooncakes. Right?"

"I am not worried," Grandpa replied with a smile. "His will be but one opinion in the end. You should remember, Mei and Yun, that not even the most powerful person in the world can diminish your true value. To some animals, a silkworm is nothing but a tasty morsel, yet its silk creations adorn the palace of China."

The twins nodded, though they did not understand Grandpa's words completely. "Listen," gasped Mei. "I hear horses!"

They hurried to join the curious crowd. The sound of galloping hoofs *clip-clopped* in the distance. The ground rumbled faintly. A dust cloud appeared on the horizon and slowly grew larger, until four chestnut-colored horses emerged from the haze. Behind the horses was a bronze-plated chariot adorned with silk tassels. Yun wondered how many days they'd been riding and began calculating the distance and time in quiet whispers to Mei. Mei wondered what dangers the prince and his entourage had encountered along the way, and was reminded of childhood stories of the Monkey King, a mischievous monkey warrior who had gone on a legendary journey to the west with three other individuals. Throughout the journey, the group faced many challenging trials, including demon tricksters and stormy weather.

A humorous idea occurred to Mei. *Maybe we're the first trial,* she thought as two officials stepped down from the chariot. Each wore formal robes and a somber expression.

"Villagers of Pearl River," one of the officials announced,

"we present His Imperial Majesty's Son, the Second Son, Prince of China."

After the applause faded, the emperor's son stepped out in a flourish of golden robes. He surprised Mei and Yun by how delicate he looked. The men in the village had brown, hardened bodies from years of working under the hot sun, but the skin of the emperor's son was pale and soft, like jasmine petals.

His commanding voice, however, left little doubt about his authority. "Thank you for hosting me," he said. "It is always a pleasure to visit the lesser-known parts of China. I was advised to come to this village after hearing about its incredible mooncakes. I seek the one who makes them, an old man by the name of Wu."

Murmurs rippled through the crowd. Grandpa stepped forward. He bowed before the emperor's son.

"We are humbled His Majesty's Son came all the way to visit our village," Grandpa said. "We normally wait until the very end of the celebration to eat the mooncakes, as is our village's tradition. Please, join us for our dinner and festivities first."

"Very well." The prince nodded and patiently raised his hands, as if to say, *Begin*.

The villagers dutifully led him to the square. They went through their customary celebrations, though with less enthusiasm than normal. People sang what were supposed to be cheerful songs in a manner suitable for funerals. Nobody danced much, either. None of the children were dazzled by the brilliant firecrackers.

The emperor's son seemed puzzled by the unusual atmosphere.

"Is this what a village party is typically like?" Yun heard the prince whisper to his officials.

The food was not much better than the celebrations. Farmer Jao had refused to bring his usual roast pig, saying he'd lost too much money over the years by offering his prized pigs for the wretched festivities instead of selling them. The other families' shared dishes were lackluster, too—the flavors bland and tasteless, the vegetables limp, as if the families had cooked them begrudgingly and with minimal effort. Luckily, Grandpa's fish stew was excellent. The prince gulped it down with fervor. Mei and Yun kept a close watch, and saw him smile twice so far. Afterward, he approached Grandpa, and the two of them chuckled as they discussed the remoteness of the village.

"We had the worst weather follow us down here," the prince said, glancing at the evening sky. "Dark swirling clouds and rainstorms. The horses refused to move at one point."

He hiccupped, then said,

"When light lives and darkness dies,
There the fallen fails to rise."

He paused. "Oh dear. Did I just say that aloud? I'm becoming tongue-tied as the night goes on."

"Not to worry," Grandpa said with a nod toward the rice wine in the prince's hand. "Happens with the festivities. Yes, the climate in the mountains can sometimes be unpredictable, although I must confess I haven't seen these kinds of rolling clouds before."

"Well, it *is* the night of the full moon. Some ancient lunar magic, perhaps, if you believe the folktales." The prince grinned.

Four, five more smiles.

"You're losing the bet," Mei whispered to Yun. She felt her skin prickle the way it did before something big happened. "But because I'm nice, I'll allow you to eat your dessert tonight. Just not any for the rest of the week, because those will go to me."

"How generous," replied Yun, his mouth stuffed full of stew. "But that's not the wager anymore, remember?"

Finally, it was time for the famous mooncakes.

Grandpa's expression had been more or less pleasant the entire night. Now, as the mooncakes were being passed out one by one, he looked as serious as the officials.

"Friends, neighbors, before you eat these cakes, I want to say a few words," he said. "I know that some of us have not been feeling quite right these past few days. I say to those folks especially, I hope the mooncakes bring you relief. As always, I've put a lot of thought and effort into making these, and I am honored to share them with you tonight."

Once all the villagers had a mooncake in their hand, everyone waited for Grandpa's signal. Mei grinned in anticipation. Yun started chewing his fingernails again.

"I have worked my magic into them. Small magic, nothing too fancy," Grandpa added as the emperor's son gave him a dubious look. "Only meant to bring harmony and joy. All of you have contributed to this magic, though you may not know it. The best magic comes from within." He held up one finger. "And now . . . you may eat!"

The twins eagerly bit into their flower-shaped mooncakes.

"Argh!" gasped Mei, her eyes suddenly streaming with tears. Next to her, Yun took a careful nibble of his mooncake, then promptly turned red.

All around them, the other villagers had similar reactions. *"Aiyah!"* people cried, spitting out the pastries.

The mooncakes, which were supposed to be sweet, tasted like rotten eggs with a side of soot. Not only that, but after taking a bite, each individual felt an unmistakable sense of dread run through them. Suddenly, every unpleasant thought in the villagers' minds magnified tenfold. And then, the poisonous words began flying.

"Wu should've let one of *us* make the mooncakes instead!" yelled Madam Hu. "Why does that old fool always have to hog the spotlight?"

"He always *claims* to know what's best," chimed in Doctor Po. "Sometimes he even gives me unsolicited advice in my dreams while I sleep!"

"Does anyone have water?" rasped Elder Liu. "I'm choking!"

"The old man is trying to poison us!" others chimed in.

For a few moments, chaos reigned. Adults argued. Small children chucked their mooncakes at one another, and were soon covered in sticky crumbs. Mothers scolded them. Several rowdy teenagers set off unplanned firecrackers, adding more chaos. Someone slipped on a mooncake and fell face-first into a pile of dirt. Someone else knocked over a paper lantern, which was engulfed in flames before being stamped out by a furious Madam Hu.

Grandpa appeared stunned. Mei and Yun tried to get everyone to calm down, to no avail.

Then the noise in the crowd slowly faded. All faces turned

to the center of the square. Everyone fell completely silent as the realization hit them.

Someone had thrown a mooncake at the emperor's son.

Crumbly pastry dripped down his hair. When he spoke, he did so softly, but his voice could barely conceal his anger. "You." He pointed at Grandpa. "Step forward."

Grandpa obeyed.

"What exactly is the meaning of this?" demanded the prince. "This mooncake tastes like earwax. Are you trying to poison us?"

"Absolutely not," Grandpa hurried to say, his voice trembling slightly. "I-I have no idea what happened. The mooncakes tasted fine when I tested them two days ago—"

"You served me mooncakes that are *two days* old?"

The crowd muttered angrily.

"His Majesty's Son misunderstands," Grandpa pleaded. "Two days is what the recipe calls for. It takes two days for these mooncakes to fully take form."

The prince shook his head, then blurted,

"Illusions you use, by the by,
Which rest within the cakes to dry."

He clapped his hands over his mouth in surprise. The crowd glanced at each other, puzzled.

One of the officials whispered, "Are you all right, Your Highness?"

The emperor's son nodded fervently. He paused for a long moment, and when he spoke to Grandpa again, his mouth seemed to struggle with the words.

"You—you told us you use magic in these mooncakes. Do you deny this?"

"Yes, they do contain traces of magic, but it's supposed to be good magic."

"Then why I am suddenly speaking in—in riddles?"

"With all due respect, you did that even before you tried the mooncake."

The prince scrunched his eyebrows, as if unsure what to make of the old man quivering before him.

"Villagers of Pearl River," he said at last, addressing the public. "You know each other better than I do. Does anyone have anything to say in this old man's defense?"

Mei and Yun expected the others to chime in about how this was all a big misunderstanding. About how Grandpa was a good man, who cooked spectacular meals. But nobody spoke.

"Anyone? . . . That settles it," said the prince, turning to his officials. "Arrest him and take him to the palace. Let's see what my father says."

"No, he's innocent!" blurted Yun. His voice came out much shakier and quieter than he'd intended. He turned to his sister for help. Mei, usually the brash one, tried to say something, but her mouth went dry.

Either way, two children's voices could not have overcome the crowd's deafening silence. The two officials grabbed Grandpa's arms and led him to a rear compartment of the chariot. At that, Mei let out a cry. Yun jumped forward and tried to pull Grandpa back, but in the dim light and amidst the jostling, he mistook one of the officials' sleeves for his grandfather's. The man tossed Yun back as if he were one of the toddlers' rag dolls.

The rest of the night passed in a blur. Mei and Yun didn't remember much—only that there was a scuffle after Yun fell, and a lot of adults yelling, and a lot of blame thrown around for how the celebration turned out. As he stepped into the front compartment of the chariot, the emperor's son commented that it was the oddest festival he'd attended. ("But can you really expect much from peasants?" one of the officials answered.) Grandpa called out something about the moon to the twins, but they couldn't hear him over the commotion. The chariot pulled away in a cloud of dust. Farmer Jao suggested they deal with all this in the morning. The villagers left for their homes, grumbling as they went, leaving the decorations behind like discarded trash. The moon disappeared behind the thick clouds. A howling gust of wind extinguished the remaining lanterns. The twins found themselves left in the dark, alone.

CHAPTER FIVE

五

The Revenge

When Lotus's son was learning to walk, her husband was suddenly called in by the city magistrate and arrested.

"We have evidence that you intend to assassinate the Emperor of China," the magistrate reported.

Gardener Wong was shocked. "That's ridiculous!" he exclaimed. "I bear no ill will toward His Majesty."

"That's not what the evidence shows, unfortunately."

With that, the magistrate produced several letters supposedly drafted by the gardener. Each one went into elaborate detail on ways to kill the emperor. The magistrate also presented the gardener several small satchels of crushed herbs.

"These toxic herbs are from a rare flower only a gardener would recognize," the magistrate said suspiciously. "If ingested, they can kill a grown man. The Noble General found these in your household, along with the letters, while you and your family were out in the public gardens."

"I've never seen these before in my life," said the baffled gardener.

"Very well. We'll conduct an investigation. Meanwhile, you are under arrest for suspected treason."

And the penalty for treason was death.

The gardener insisted he was innocent. Most of the city was shocked when they heard the charges brought against him. "He's a kind man," they argued at first. "He wouldn't hurt a housefly."

"Nonsense," retorted the Noble General. "He mutilates perfectly good trees all the time, and stinks up the air with animal waste!"

"Isn't that just pruning and using fertilizer?" a boy piped up. But his sensible questions were drowned out by the Noble General's loud rants in the city courtyard.

"We cannot live peacefully in this city knowing a traitor is in our midst! Today he plots against the emperor; tomorrow, it could be your own children. He could poison the trees and flowers he grows so that anyone who breathes them will get sick. Do you want your lives ruled by that kind of fear?" The Noble General summoned his fiercest look and pointed at the people. "Those of you who disagree must have something to hide. I should tell the magistrate to look into you, too!"

By the end of the day, most people agreed that the gardener was guilty.

The magistrate, easily persuaded by the fearful mood of the people and by the pressure of the nobleman, decided that was all the confirmation he needed. He sentenced the gardener to death the next morning. When Lotus heard the news, her face went ashen. She presented herself to the magistrate and pleaded on her husband's behalf. But her words, however sharp and impressive, were no match against the mounting evidence and the other residents' misguided suspicions. Nor were they a match against the Noble General's powerful authority and influence.

Her husband was executed before dawn.

"Normally, a traitor's entire family would be killed as well," the Noble General told her with a sneer. "Lucky for you, I have asked the emperor to pardon you and your son. However, you must be punished for defending a guilty man."

Lotus's punishment, ordered by the Noble General, was to have her precious hair cut short. Back then, nobody cut their hair; it was seen as severing a part of one's own body. None of the animals of the earth trimmed their hair, after all. For someone like Lotus to have her long, gleaming hair cut short was both humiliating and a tragedy.

Grief-stricken by her husband's murder and desperate for guidance, Lotus turned to the only being who might help. She bundled up her baby and fled to the mountains outside the city. The air was cold against her bare neck. The path was arduous, and mud and rocks clung to her heels, gripping her every step of the way as she ascended the uneven terrain. Hours later, her teeth clenching and her mind focused on uplifting words like "accomplish," "determination," "perseverance," she finally made it to the summit of the first mountain outside the city.

There, she raised her head to the moon and called upon a mystical creature that had been whispered about in folklore for hundreds of generations.

There was no reply. Her baby shifted in her arms and began to wail from the cold. Lotus comforted him as she awaited an answer from above.

Just when the night reached its deepest chill and Lotus had nearly given up hope, the shadows on the moon shifted. A bright light fell upon the mountaintop. A white rabbit rose out of the pool of moonlight and stood in front of Lotus. It was the Jade Rabbit, inhabitant of the moon. The Jade Rabbit was a small creature—the tips of its ears barely reached Lotus's knees—but it contained more magic in its front paws than did half the world.

"Please help me," Lotus begged. "My husband was killed, and my heart is heavier than a storm cloud."

The Jade Rabbit twitched its whiskers. It normally did not intervene in human affairs. But it took pity on the woman and her infant.

"I cannot help you exact revenge or carry out justice," the Jade Rabbit replied. "However, I will grant you some of my powers from the moon, so that your heart may heal."

"Yes, please, you are very kind," wept Lotus.

A few moments later, the magical creature produced a glistening vial. "A single drop of this elixir is more valuable than all the silver in China. It brings language to life and will guarantee you and your child many blissful years to come." The Jade Rabbit handed the vial to Lotus. "Drink it and think of soothing words," it instructed. "Words like 'peace,' 'prosperity,' and 'happiness.' Do you understand?"

Lotus took the vial and drank the liquid. A warm, tingling sensation spread over her body, all the way into her fingertips. She could feel a power growing inside her, bursting to be released. She smiled dreamily.

Then, an instant later, her smile vanished.

"Words, my dear rabbit, are what I'm best at," she responded quietly.

CHAPTER SIX

六

Disappearing Act

There's a saying that once you hit rock bottom, you can't go any lower—that things can't get any worse, they can only get better. Of course, this analogy works only if you've actually hit rock bottom, and not something like quicksand, which continues to pull you farther into unpleasant depths.

Mei and Yun felt they had sunk into never-ending quicksand.

Sometime in the night after the disastrous festival, the moon completely wiped itself from the sky and never came back, not even after the clouds finally drifted away. The disappearance of the moon was followed by a sudden, sunless heat wave that gripped the village, so hot that the ground was scorched. As dawn approached a few hours later, the heat was lifted by a snowstorm that pelted every crop in the fields.

The villagers had never seen such a thing. They looked on from their windows in horror. Shivering farmers frantically tried to save their crops and livestock in the morning. Animals froze and keeled over in the snow.

The twins hid inside their home, trying to figure out their next step amidst all the confusion. Neither sibling had slept all night. Like everyone else, they'd stayed up watching the bizarre events unfold outside their window. In the pitch-black darkness, they thought they saw wisps of bright and dark green smoke rising from both the ground and the other villagers' windows. They'd observed green strands like this once before, when one of the village kids had dozed off by the river and woken up yelling. It was not a good sign.

"It's sabotage!" Yun said for the thirty-fourth time that afternoon. His eyes were bloodshot as he paced their bedroom, his mind whirring at top speed. "Someone poisoned Grandpa's mooncakes. I bet it was Madam Hu, that jealous busybody—"

Madam Hu was not the first suspect on Yun's list. Every other villager was also a candidate, all the way down to the toddlers. ("*They* were probably the ones who tossed the mooncakes at the emperor's son's head!" fumed Yun.)

"What about the snowstorm?" piped up Mei, who was curled tight under the covers with her eyes shut. Part of her still believed it all was a bad dream (a very realistic bad dream), and she thought if she closed her eyes long enough, everything might go back to normal. "And the moon disappearing?" she added. "No villager could have done that. Could it be . . . could it be punishment from the emperor's son himself, like the neighbors said? As in, *he* controlled the weather?"

Earlier that morning, Mei had tried to visit several of the villagers, only to have doors shut in her face. The nicer ones said the terrible weather made it impossible to do anything about the previous night's events. The not-so-nice ones outright blamed Grandpa for everything. "He angered the prince, and now our village is being punished!" they'd shouted.

Mei poked her head out from under her covers and looked at Yun. "On second thought, I take that back about the prince and the snowstorm," she said. "It would be strange that a man who seems to barely get enough sunlight could control the weather with such force."

Yun agreed. He deduced it wasn't the work of the emperor's son, but something bigger.

"Think about it," he said. "If someone from the imperial court had such powers, wouldn't everyone across China already know about it?"

He sifted through the messy pile of scrolls he'd taken from his father's collection. They were from Baba's old days in the Imperial City—copies of mandates, historical records, and notes on palace regulations. Yun had spent the morning studying them feverishly, looking up rules of the imperial court and how to challenge an arrest, and searching for any similar strange weather patterns from history. So far, he hadn't come across anything like it.

"It *is* odd that the weird weather started after they took Grandpa, isn't it?" asked Mei. "That was when the moon vanished into thin air."

"The weird weather started the day before the festival with the rolling clouds," Yun corrected her. "Either way, something as big as the moon disappearing can wreak havoc on nature. As it already has."

"It must not be just our village, then? The effects of the moon would alter the entire country, right?"

Yun rubbed his forehead in thought. He had a suspicion—just an inkling, but nonetheless a strong one—that the neighbors had been partially right; that the odd weather was indeed only affecting their village. But saying so was neither helpful nor useful, as he had no way to confirm it.

For the rest of the day, they studied maps and outlined futile plan after futile plan to rescue their grandpa. The Imperial City was a month away by foot, more than one week on horseback. No matter how much the twins brainstormed, the journey seemed next to impossible—especially since the only horses in the village had died in the storm. Outside, the afternoon waned and the sky grew dark. They huddled around the brazier in their bedroom for warmth and light, reading under the dim orange glow of the ember rocks inside.

Late in the evening, Yun lit a small lamp and headed to the kitchen. Smelly Tail was curled underneath the table, trying to stay warm in the sudden winter. When she saw Yun, she leapt toward him and whined, clearly distraught by the unusual happenings. Yun rummaged through the cupboards for something to feed the cat.

Sh-sh-sh-sh. A rattling noise made Yun stop.

He heard it again. *Sh-rat-a-tat-a-tat-sh-sh.*

It was coming from the shelf where Grandpa kept his jars and spices. Yun went closer. There he saw a porcelain jar shaking on the shelf.

It was a pretty jar. The outside was white with delicate artwork painted in blue glaze, one of those elaborate designs that looked like random swirls from afar but were actually detailed drawings up close, of blossoms and birds and dragons. It was Grandpa's favorite jar; he usually kept it displayed on the shelf in his room, and had often told the twins that out of all the things in their small house, the jar was the only item off-limits to them. Out of respect for Grandpa, Mei and Yun did not play with the jar, though unbeknownst to the others, Yun had peeked inside once or twice. The jar had always been empty, leading him to conclude it was likely a decorative memento of some sort.

But now it was shaking side to side on the shelf in the kitchen, as if an earthquake was causing it to move. Yun grabbed the jar and plucked off the lid.

He stifled a gasp.

"Mei!" he yelled. "Come quick!"

A few seconds later, Mei stumbled into the kitchen, rubbing her eyes. "I'm not very hungry," she said. "I can't think about food at a time like—"

"No, look!"

Inside the porcelain jar were puffs of gray substance, with swirling threads of black and green.

"Those look familiar," whispered Mei. "Aren't those the—?"

"They don't look anything like *this*." Yun clamped the lid back on.

The contents looked like the mysterious, colorful vapors the twins had grown up seeing around the village their whole lives. Yet the wisps they saw were often gold or blue, like the sky on a pleasant day. The ones in the jar, meanwhile, looked more like the underside of a miniature storm cloud, and just as turbulent. Parts of the cloud glowed bright, followed by a thunderous rattle that nearly made Yun drop the jar.

"Isn't that the jar Grandpa always keeps locked in his room?" asked Mei.

"Yes. I found it just now on the kitchen shelf. He must've put it there yesterday..."

Mei stared at the shaking jar. Her eyes grew wide. "Do you think," she said in a hushed tone, "that *this* is Grandpa's secret ingredient?"

"Secret ingredient?"

"For the mooncakes."

Yun snuck another peek inside the jar. The tiny storm cloud glowed and thundered. "This doesn't look like anything that could go into food."

"But he talked about using *magic* in the mooncakes, remember?"

"That was just a metaphor, Mei."

But even as Yun said it, they both knew the jar contained something not quite of this world, something extraordinary.

Neither said anything for several long minutes. Outside, the wind howled. A cup clattered to the floor. The noise jolted them from their thoughts.

"Whatever it is, it's not important right now," said Mei. "We have to get to the Imperial City and rescue Grandpa. We can tell people there about what's happening to the village." She opened the window shutters to peek outside, where snow continued to fall.

It wasn't clear how the rest of the villagers were faring.

Mei and Yun could see lights in their neighbors' windows, glowing fires and dimly lit lanterns. Nobody was outside. Earlier in the day, Mei and Yun had overheard Doctor Po and several other men shouting that they would be leaving to get help from outside the village, as soon as the snowstorm wound down.

"We do have to leave the village," Yun agreed, putting the jar carefully on the ground. "But not for the Imperial City. First, I think we should go somewhere closer to get help."

"But what about Grandpa?"

As if in answer to Mei's question, another gust of wind shrieked like a teakettle and shook the window shutters.

"Going somewhere closer is the only way we can get help fast," Yun said solemnly. "The snow isn't letting up anytime soon. I'd be surprised if Doctor Po and his men leave tomorrow. Even if they do, there's no way they'd take us along, and then nobody else would know about Grandpa's plight. It's up to us."

"You're right," grumbled Mei, wrapping her arms around her body. "I suppose if we don't try to help our village first, everyone's dying thought will be of how Grandpa caused all this." Her teeth chattered, partially from the cold, partially from uneasiness. "Let's sleep on it, and then say the first plan that comes to our minds in the morning," she finally said. "Whatever it is, we'll do it."

To an outsider, it might seem a rather odd way to make a decision, but the twins often shared what they called a connected sixth sense—the kind of intuition twins understand. It was responsible for the times Mei knew her brother's thoughts before he spoke them aloud, and likewise the times

Yun finished his sister's sentences. After a good night's sleep, Mei and Yun were almost always on the same page when they awoke, and for this reason, they liked making decisions together this way—when they both agreed on something, neither needed to explain themselves.

That night, as it sometimes happened, the twins had the same dream. Often enough, the dream would be about something trivial—an argument they'd left off earlier that day, for instance, or the conclusion to a game or sword fight. On this night, the dream was far more somber, but it was a familiar dream, one they'd had many times since their parents' departure.

In their dream, their parents were alive and well, but they were as ghosts—not quite belonging to this world. They stood opposite the twins on an unfamiliar street. Both Mei and Yun tried to run to them, calling out, "Mama! Baba!" only to have their cries swallowed by thick fog. They could never get close enough for their parents to hear or notice them.

Only this time, Grandpa was in the dream, too. He stood next to them, there but not quite there, and said calmly, "In the city lies your answer."

When they woke up in the early morning, the twins knew what they had to do.

They would go to the City of Ashes.

·✳·

It wasn't a completely ridiculous plan. As Yun pointed out, the City of Ashes was technically the closest place to their village, and it was on the way to the Imperial City. There, they could see if they could hitch a ride from someone heading to the palace. And if not, they could at least notify someone that their village had succumbed to a flash blizzard, burying all the crops and animals.

"Unless the city's in an even worse state than our village," he added, highlighting the unease they were both feeling. In order for the twins to believe that they could actually get assistance in the City of Ashes, they first had to convince themselves the rumors about the city were hogwash. And that was much easier said than done.

When the twins were nine, about three years after Mama and Baba had left, Grandpa departed one weekend to run some errands. Grandpa didn't reveal the details of his trip, but he had gone on similar trips before, to get supplies from larger towns or to visit friends he knew who lived in the mountains. In his absence, the twins had stayed at Madam Hu's. By Sunday afternoon, they'd had their fill of Madam Hu's questions and proclamations, and they'd pretended to doze off in the bedroom while Madam Hu and several of her friends chatted in the living room.

That was when they overheard whispers about Grandpa's trip.

"Don't know what he expects," Madam Hu had tutted. "Made the same trip two years in a row already. The City of Ashes is as haunted as a tomb. Soon as his daughter and that husband of hers announced they were headed over there, I knew they were goners."

The others murmured in agreement.

"What were they thinking?" said Mrs. Po.

"Oh, the son-in-law was one of those scholar types, you know," answered Madam Hu. "Always hungry for information. He worked up at the palace for a brief period before traveling down this way and meeting Wu's daughter. They had a lot in common, those two. They were both interested in history and ancient ruins, that kind of awful stuff. Said they were 'intrigued' by the mysteries of the City of Ashes and wanted to see it for themselves. I say, the only real mystery is why some people have no practical sense!"

"So you think they're really . . . *gone* then?" Madam Lilian whispered.

"Lilian, it's been three years. Same thing happened to a neighbor of a cousin of mine, who lives on the other side of the mountains. Neighbor went to the city, hoping to do some business, and was never heard from again."

At this point, Mei and Yun had sat upright and were staring at each other in stunned silence.

"What happened the last time Old Wu went?" someone else asked.

"Didn't you hear?" Madam Hu lowered her voice, and Mei and Yun inched closer to the bedroom door to hear what came next.

According to Madam Hu, Grandpa had borrowed one of Farmer Jao's horses, then headed off into the steep mountain trails toward the City of Ashes. When he'd arrived at the city gates, however, the entrance was locked. There had been no guards in sight. He'd waited until nearly another day passed, when he had no choice but to return home.

"Same thing happened the first time he went," Madam Hu finished. "I'd give up if I were him. Probably a good thing the gates don't open, if you ask me. You don't want to go in there and face whatever awaits you."

Until that day, the twins had been too young to grasp the true significance of their parents' absence and how little Grandpa really knew. In the tales he used to tell them about the City of Ashes, the city had supposedly been barricaded by a high-ranking general after its downfall, and anybody who tried to enter would be punished. Their parents, unlike most people, did not believe in the rumored curses of forbidden walls, unseen voices, and empty streets. Neither did Grandpa. In fact, it was their steadfast rejection of the rumors that had consoled Mei and Yun all these years. Whenever other people spoke of the city's supposed horrors, the twins would smile secretly at each other because they alone shared inside knowledge. They had their trusted grandfather, who assured them again and again, "Your parents are busy; they will be staying in the city for a few more months," and Mei and Yun would casually accept the fact before going back to their reading or dueling or arguing.

That weekend at Madam Hu's had marked the first time they understood an inkling of the truth. Like a tangram puzzle, all the pieces suddenly began to fit to form a coherent picture. To date, they'd never received a letter from their parents. All this time, Grandpa could not possibly have known what Mama and Baba were up to. Grandpa, their trusted guardian who was like a third parent to them, was in the dark like everyone else. He had gone to the City of Ashes, looking for answers.

Since then, seeing no reason not to do the same, the twins had tried several times to sneak to the city to find out what had happened to their parents. But Grandpa always seemed to know what they were planning and caught them even before they reached the entrance to the village. Because they couldn't outright disobey or lie to Grandpa, they made a secret pact that once they were of age, they'd make a trip to the City of Ashes no matter what.

But now, Grandpa wasn't there. They were all alone.

It was time for the trip.

·☀·

Twenty minutes later, Mei read off the packing list in the kitchen.

"Boots?"

"Check," answered Yun.

"Knife?"

"Check."

"Blanket?"

"Check."

"Bandages, water jug, lantern?"

"Check, check, check."

"Hm." Mei looked up. "We should take some leftover buns for food, too."

When the buns were packed, the twins peered outside the window. The snow had stopped. The early morning sun had come out, painting the pale blue sky with shades of pink and orange. It looked almost deceptively peaceful.

"One more thing." Yun grabbed Grandpa's porcelain jar from the floor and placed it inside his duffel bag with their other equipment.

"Why are you taking that?" asked Mei.

"I don't know. Maybe it'll come in handy."

The twins bid farewell to Smelly Tail and cracked open

the window for her. Yun spent several minutes mixing a fish-and-rice leftover dish and set it on the floor. It was the same dish they'd often seen their mother make in the middle of the night for the cat, when the rest of the family had fallen asleep.

"We'll be back," Mei promised. "Until then, you'll have to make do with this, and mice."

Then they left the house. The village was quiet. Every house was covered by a thick layer of snow. Nobody else had come outside yet. There were no tracks on the path; even the village outhouse was undisturbed.

Mei and Yun trudged through the snow, huddled inside their winter jackets, stiff with multiple patches from years of mending. Their breaths made clouds of fog in the air. The cold sank into their skin, and they drew closer to the small, iron-clad coal burner that Yun carried—a traveling pocket heater, to sustain them for the journey. By the time they reached the river, which had frozen white like the willow trees along the banks, their cheeks were numb. They wondered what it was like the morning their parents had left so long ago. Had they been scared? Determined? Excited?

Yun knelt beside the river to fill their travel jugs with water that still ran below the surface. As he tapped on the ice, Mei stood still. "Wait a minute," she said as she stared into the distance.

Something didn't seem right. She went to the nearest willow tree and carefully climbed her way up. The tree was much more slippery when it was frozen. Bits of snow and ice sprinkled the air as she clutched the icy branches, but she found her footing and soon was near the top. There, she looked into the distance again. A single, frosty-white path ran through the hills and mountains surrounding the village.

"There's a trail of snow," she called down to Yun. "But everything else around it is untouched."

Yun squinted in the direction his sister pointed. "Impossible," he started, but even with his blurry vision, he could make out the unscathed green trees as far as the eye could see. It was as if a giant creature had walked off carrying an enormous, leaky bucket of snow, sprinkling it along its way and nowhere else.

"It's like the weather followed someone—or something," Mei whispered. "Right here to our village."

"Or away from it," Yun added. "Can you see where the snow leads?"

Mei's eyes followed the strange snow trail, watched it wind through the hills here and there, until it came to a stop. She nodded.

"You know," she said slowly. "I'm starting to think that city is cursed after all."

CHAPTER SEVEN

七

The Curse

*O*n the night Lotus drank the elixir, a series of odd, rolling clouds swept over the City of Blossoms. Shortly after, the moon vanished suddenly from the sky. That was when everything went downhill.

Blossom trees wilted. Here and there, people randomly disappeared from their beds. Storm after storm raged: hailstorms and thunderstorms and snowstorms. In between the storms, houses caught on fire for no apparent reason, trapping those inside. At one point, there was a dry spell on the city for two months straight, and flames raged in every corner until the sky was bloodred. The blazes stripped the gilded linings off rooftops until the city lost all its glitter, and ashes and corpses piled the streets.

At the heart of it all was Lotus, who had come to possess

a powerful magic the likes of which no one had ever seen. Her words, once enchanting on paper, now seemed to gain a life of their own. She walked around the city with her baby in her arms and recited her poetry to passersby with a solemn look on her face.

One of her poems went as such:

"The birds, let them carry
The sorrows of the skies
And bring them to this city
To swallow the sunrise."

The next moment, hundreds of black crows closed in on the city. When they finally left, the sun did not rise for three days.

The Noble General had fled the city the very first day after Lotus returned from the mountaintop. Most people were not sure what had happened to him, only that his house had been set aflame, and that he barely managed to escape by jumping out the window, hopping on his horse, and galloping off in the direction of the Imperial City. But I saw Lotus standing quietly in his garden before the inferno as she spoke:

"You will speak in riddles
Until the end of time,
Confused, like a babbling frog.
The skies will rain suffering
Should you or your descendants return."

Others fled the city, too. Some families decided to stay, thinking the events would surely end. They locked their shutters and placed bowls of goldfish on their doorsteps for good luck. By that point, none of the city officials were left to take charge. Lotus, powerful beyond belief, became the de facto ruler of the city. Some were drawn to her power and tried to follow and serve her, partially so they'd be spared from her wrath, partially in the vain hopes of sharing some of that power. Others simply feared her.

The storms and fires eventually stopped, but then the curse took another turn. As time went on, there came a period when the sky was cloudy for months on end, and people became unusually frightened, then morose, then frightened again, as if trapped in a never-ending nightmare. Neighbors came to distrust one another. No one helped when someone else was in need. A strange weight descended upon the people of the city. Their fears, multiplied by the magic, enfolded the area and slowly detached the people from the physical world.

Through it all, Lotus's anger continued to burn. Anger is one of those emotions that fuels itself, growing bigger and fiercer until it extinguishes everything in its path, yet it is still never satisfied. It very soon became clear the magic was consuming Lotus from within. She found she was not content with the Noble General's hasty departure, nor was she pleased with the curse she'd cast upon him. She tried to hunt him down to the place he'd fled, but discovered that, try as she might, she physically could not. Her fury against the City of Blossoms, whose citizens had betrayed her husband, now turned on itself and tethered her, ironically, to the very place and people she detested. She was unable to leave. It was as if an invisible wall blocked her path. Her emotions, like rain, drenched the premises but no farther.

On the advice of the Noble General, who had managed to reach his old home in the Imperial City, the emperor sent troops down to the City of Blossoms to barricade it with a real wall.

Lotus did not stop them. She gathered her son and a few possessions and took refuge in one of the temples after shooing out the monks who lived there. She did not venture outside again.

Months stretched to years. The city crumbled into disarray. Its inhabitants had now completely separated from the present world and become trapped in the past. Lotus, too, became a relic in time.

Officials from the emperor's palace passed a law forbidding anyone from venturing to the desolate place that was now known as the City of Ashes.

CHAPTER EIGHT

八

Before the Gates

The trail of snow led right to the City of Ashes. By the time Mei and Yun reached the gates, it was nightfall.

Oddly enough, their journey had been smoother than expected. There had been no sudden blizzards or heat waves. The previous snowfall had rendered the forest in the mountains still and quiet, without even the faintest rustling of leaves. The twins had thought the snow would make it difficult to trek, but if anything, the crusty layer cushioned the steep mountain trails and made it easier to hike, like walking on a thick quilt that protected against jagged steps and sharp falls. They'd followed the snowy path, winding their way through trees and brambles, until they reached the city walls. It was easy, much easier than the fabled Mountain of Ten Thousand Steps in the north. The path of snow had guided their way like the North Star.

It helped, too, that the twins knew the area well. They'd foraged the mountains before, collecting wild mushrooms with Grandpa or gathering herbs for Doctor Po. Mei and Yun also had excellent navigational skills. Mei had a natural sense of direction; she was one of those people who could travel to a brand-new place miles away while simultaneously memorizing the entire way back. Yun, meanwhile, knew his way around by relying on all sorts of miscellaneous knowledge, like the fact that moss grew on the north side of trees, or that all waters flowed downstream. Together, the twins rarely got lost.

And perhaps a little bit of whatever caused the recent events—the magic, the unnatural forces—had factored into their trip, so that time and distance had been shortened for the twelve-year-olds.

(But I am merely speculating.)

The twins now stood in the moonless night before the thick iron doors, around ten times their height and nearly just as wide. Grayish yellow walls stretched out on either side of the sealed doors. The fortress surrounded the city on all sides, making it impossible for even an army of grown soldiers to climb.

"I guess this is what Grandpa was up against," said Mei.

"Hello?" shouted Yun. His voice echoed in the vast emptiness.

"Anyone home?" called Mei.

The twins called out several more times, to no avail.

"You're sure you can't climb those walls?" Yun asked his sister.

"You can't be serious."

"It shouldn't be that much different than climbing a tree, right?" Yun caught Mei's furious expression. "Never mind."

"I knew this was a bad idea," sighed Mei. She shivered; all the coals in their pocket heater had nearly burned up. "Let's set up camp for the night and go home first thing in the morning."

"No, there must be a way in." Yun closed his eyes and thought hard. Suddenly, an idea hit him.

He fumbled for a match, then lit the small gas lantern they'd packed. Guided by the circle of orange flame, he moved slowly alongside the stone wall, his hands touching the rough stone surface. Toward the corner of the fortress, he knelt and examined the bottom closely. *Aha!* A tiny hole was burrowed under the wall, large enough for a small dog to crawl through. No doubt the people who built the wall did not consider tiny animals as a threat.

Yun kicked away the snow at his feet. The frosted ground below it was hard as rocks. He dug out the knife from his duffel bag and carved the blade into the ground. The dirt crumbled.

"I've got it!" he called to Mei.

They both dug at the ground with tools they had brought—knife, spoons, and eventually their hands. Their fingers stung from digging in the cold, but an hour later there was a small crater beneath the hole, just large enough for two skinny children to squeeze through.

"Bet the other kids will stop making fun of us for being wimpy now, when they hear we saved them by going to the City of Ashes," Mei remarked after they wriggled and twisted inside the wall to the other side. They dusted off the dirt that clung to their fingers the best they could, then looked at their new surroundings.

The inside of the fabled city walls was completely black. The light from their lantern cast long, distorted shadows of the twins along the long, dark street. Dark and *deserted* street. No one else seemed to be there.

Mei and Yun instinctively huddled close together. At least they were not alone, they reminded themselves quietly. In spooky tales, monsters always came after the lone protagonist— a lost little girl in the woods or a boy wandering on his own. Down the street were dim outlines of buildings, so faint they blended with the inky night. The twins slowly began walking.

Inside the gated city were more gates. Yun and Mei had read that in many cities across China, the houses were arranged around private courtyards, like mini neighborhoods. They passed several blocks of such dwellings, each neighborhood surrounded by windowless walls and one closed gate. If anybody had been living behind these walls, there were no signs to indicate their presence. Some of the walls were half crumbled, revealing houses with missing rooftops and broken foundations behind them.

Yun tried one of the gates. Locked. Same with the next four.

"Mama and Baba might be in one of these neighborhoods," he whispered in response to Mei's questioning gaze.

Something caught in Mei's throat. She cleared it, then said with a trace of defiance, "Probably. Seems like everyone's home asleep, though."

Deep down, both twins weren't sure how they'd feel seeing their parents again after all these years. Joy, certainly. Or maybe they'd just feel angry and betrayed that they'd left in the first place. That was why Mei didn't like to think about it too long, and why Yun felt the need to overanalyze it.

It was indeed a strange city to visit on a whim, even for a curious scholar like their father. According to the rumors, they were supposed to hear wailing and other noises in the walled city. But now, there was only silence coming from all directions. Still, it was very true that the place felt haunted, from the seemingly empty houses to the lack of noises. What's more, every little draft brushed their skin with a ghostlike sigh, making their spines tingle and their hair stand up. Now and then, the twins glanced over their shoulders.

They turned onto a new street. That was when they saw the first shadow approaching.

Mei was the first to see it with her sharp vision. She froze mid-step and clutched Yun's arm.

"What?" asked Yun.

"Don't move." Mei trembled.

Yun squinted into the distance, but he couldn't make out anything in the dark. He hated being nearsighted in times like this.

"Why?" he whispered in alarm. "What do you see?"

Then he saw the figure, too. An old man in a cloak walked toward them down the street.

Encountering a stranger in the dark at night is always a bit unnerving. Doubly so, if it's in a deserted city with no one else in sight. The twins' first instinct was to drop the lantern and run in the opposite direction, but then they realized this was a person who could potentially help them.

The figure continued walking closer until the twins could clearly see his features. He had grayish white hair and wrinkles in his somber face. There was something odd about his cloak and skin—the old man looked like he was made of a thin shadowy material, as if someone had traced a drawing and didn't fully color in the lines. He did not look at the twins; instead, he looked straight ahead, as if the children didn't exist.

"Excuse me, um, sir," Mei said.

The man kept walking.

"Sir—hey, sir?" Yun tried.

They waved and called hello, but even when the man was within five inches of them, he didn't pay them the slightest attention. The twins jumped aside at the last minute so the old man wouldn't walk into them. He passed through without a single glance at either one.

Mei and Yun shared a look of bewilderment. Mei went after the old man and tapped his shoulder. But her hand felt nothing but air. The two of them watched the shadowy figure disappear past what the lantern's light could reach.

"Mei, you okay?" Yun said. His sister was still holding her hand midair. "Don't worry about him, he's old and couldn't hear or feel you."

Mei didn't want to say out loud that *she* couldn't feel the old man. "I'm fine," she warbled after a few moments.

They continued walking. Mei, however, was still shaken by her encounter. Had she touched some kind of ghost? She tried hard not to think about what else lurked in the gloom.

Something crunched under their feet. Yun lowered the lantern, then looked sick. Underneath his boot was a blackened, smiling skull.

CHAPTER NINE

九

The Moon Children

*A*nd what of Lotus's baby boy, you ask?
      For the answer to that question, we must go back to the days that followed Lotus drinking the elixir.

The Jade Rabbit was devastated when the curse began. Although it normally did not intervene in humans' problems, it knew it had indirectly caused the terrible events now plaguing the City of Blossoms. The rabbit took pity on the newly orphaned children in the city. It loved children; they did not bear grudges the way adults did, they were witty, and their smiles shone for miles around. A child without a family was a tragic thing.

So the rabbit gathered all the orphans it could and sent them out of the city's walls. Across China that year, there was a strange phenomenon known as "moon children," where kind-hearted people would stumble upon little children under the moonlight—next to a tree in the forest, or beside a grassy field, or on the doorstep of a house. These orphans were taken in and welcomed with open hearts.

The Jade Rabbit took particular pity on Lotus's baby, who lived restlessly in the temple. By that time, his mother could no longer tend to him. She was a phantom now, like the people in the city—one who lives in a dream, real yet not real, disconnected from the rest of the world.

So one moonlit night, the magical creature took him away, too. "Your mother can care for you no longer," it told him. "You do not understand it now, but revenge always destroys the people who carry it out, like a burning log that dissolves into flames."

The rabbit paused and looked at the sleeping baby. It could tell that he had a pure heart, as most children did—a heart not yet hardened by the troubles of the world.

"You've been through particular hardship, and you have your whole life ahead of you. This is what I should've done in the first place."

The Jade Rabbit pressed a paw to the baby's forehead. For a moment, the baby's skin glowed bright like the moon. Then the rabbit took him away from the city walls to a tiny village close to the mountains. It made sure the child was safe in the care of his new guardians, who came upon him bathed in a moonbeam at the base of a willow tree beside a river.

"Goodbye," the Jade Rabbit whispered before it disappeared in a sprinkle of moonlight. "I trust you will use your powers for good instead of evil."

CHAPTER TEN

✝

Ghosts and Rabbits

Mei and Yun kept walking down street after street in the desolate city. Now and then, the wind whistled through the decrepit buildings, which were most certainly empty. Save for the old man who'd passed them earlier, the twins didn't meet another soul.

Up ahead was what looked like a temple. The forlorn building was set on the top of a set of stairs and had multiple stacked roofs reaching toward the stars. But the entire temple gave off an uninviting vibe. The windows were dark, save for a single circular one at the very top that had a faint orange glow. Etched in the stone at the foot of the stairs was a single character:

火

Fire. The twins exchanged a puzzled look. Mei's skin prickled. Her eyes followed the stairs to the top, then did a double take. At the top stood several people in hooded cloaks, as still and silent as statues.

"Maybe we can ask them for help," Yun suggested.

"*No,* Yun." Mei thought again of the ghostlike old man whose shoulder she had tapped. The last people she wanted to ask were a bunch of hooded figures outside an ominous temple.

"Why not?" protested Yun, who did not know what Mei knew. "There's a lower and lower probability we'll find someone else to help us in this city."

Mei tried to tug her twin along. "Let's leave. I—"

"No, we should ask—"

Their back-and-forth jostle made Yun accidentally drop his bag. The contents spilled to the snow-covered ground.

Grandpa's porcelain jar dropped in the mess. Its lid fell off, and the flashing green-and-gray substance inside started to float out like thick smoke. Yun fumbled for the lid and tried to clamp it back on the jar, but most of the cloud had escaped. It felt like nothing but damp air.

There was a sudden swishing sound from behind them. Figures appeared out of nowhere: men, women, even small children. A moment later, the twins were surrounded by at least a dozen people. They all looked like the first old man they saw—visible yet not quite visible, the way a star in the night sky seems brighter in one's peripheral vision than looking at it straight on. Each seemed to be made of the same thin shadowy material, as if they could fade away at any second.

"W-We don't mean to h-harm anyone," Yun addressed the group shakily. "We're here to seek help."

The ghostly people did not seem to hear or see Yun. They were each absorbed in something else: one woman seemed to be laughing and chatting with another woman beside her, though neither made a sound. Three children were exchanging something invisible amongst themselves, cupping their hands and grinning. Then the closest person—a woman with a cane—walked through the mysterious floating substance from Grandpa's jar. Her features suddenly sharpened, from her graying hair to the outline of her bare feet. She blinked at the twins in alarm, seemingly noticing them for the first time.

"Ghosts." The woman held up her cane, as if to ward the twins off. "You look just like her."

Before Mei or Yun could ask who the woman was talking about, a small boy entered the cloud. Like the woman, his outline became more opaque. He gaped in surprise at the twins.

"Who're you?" he asked.

Yun cleared his throat. "Pardon us, we're from a village in the mountains," he tried again. "Our grandpa's been taken, and there was a sudden snowstorm, and—"

"You look just like her," the woman with the cane repeated, focusing her gaze on Mei. "A younger version. I see it in your face."

"Who?" asked Mei.

Wham! Without warning, the woman whacked her cane against Mei's shin. Surprisingly, it hurt quite a bit. Mei yelped.

"It was you!" the woman howled.

She raised her cane again, but the cloud had slowly dispersed, and her features faded. She opened her mouth to say something else, but no sound came out.

As the cloud passed over the others in the group, one by one their features strengthened, then faded again as the cloud moved on. Each time their features became clearer, the people gasped at the sight of Mei and Yun.

Then a bright white light shone behind the twins. They turned around to see a small glowing rabbit at their feet.

To their enormous astonishment, the rabbit spoke.

"Welcome, children. I see you have the gift."

☀

This is it, I've definitely lost my mind.

The uneasy thought ran across Mei's and Yun's heads as they followed the white rabbit toward a deserted section of the city. The rabbit shone brighter than their lantern, its fur as radiant as moonlight. If it wasn't for the alarming fact that it glowed and spoke, the twins almost certainly would have tried to pet it, as the animal looked quite fluffy and soft. It reassured them every now and then in a calm voice that "they were almost there," and that they would "have a serious talk very soon."

It was also well past the two children's bedtime, and the twins were both tired and hungry—ideal conditions for seeing mirages and things that aren't there.

The fact that they were following a talking rabbit *shouldn't* have been surprising, given everything they had witnessed in the city that night. The twins fuzzily recalled fables involving a mystical rabbit from their bedtime stories years ago. According to Chinese legend, there was a magical rabbit who lived on the moon, where it pounded the elixir of life in its jade mortar. On nights when the moon was full, one could see shadows on its golden-white surface form the faint outline of the animal's body. The Jade Rabbit could perform strong, powerful magic from the moonlight. It used its magic for good, rescuing cities from plagues, but it also had the potential to destroy populations with its powers.

In spite of all the tales they'd heard, however, never once did Mei and Yun think the rabbit was real. It was up there with the childhood stories they'd been told of the beloved Monkey King, or folktales of the mythical Nian monster who lived under the mountains. Good stories, but just stories, meant to amuse young children.

They came upon an open pasture with frozen, wilted trees. The rabbit stopped underneath one of the trees.

"This is a quiet spot. We should not be disturbed here." The creature twitched its whiskers and looked up at the twins. Its dark eyes were as luminous as the rest of its body. *"Greetings, I am the Jade Rabbit, Guardian of the Moon."*

"Hello," Mei and Yun managed to croak. As an afterthought, they gave a bow. If this was indeed a mythical guardian, it likely demanded proper respect.

The rabbit seemed to appreciate this. *"As you may know, this pasture once was the most popular place in the city. Families would take strolls and have picnics here among the many blossoming trees. That was many moons ago . . . nearly seventy years. The trees have long stopped bearing blossoms."*

The twins looked at the barren trees, like skeletons in the night. They couldn't imagine a less likely place for picnics and strolls.

"We've heard some tales," Yun said hesitantly. "Our grandpa said the city used to be lovely."

The Jade Rabbit lowered its head. *"Yes. The city used to be one of the most beautiful places on this side of the mountains. It was my personal favorite. Lush green fields, golden rooftops, flowers on every street corner. But it all ended when the curse swept through the city."*

"The curse?"

"Lotus's curse."

The Jade Rabbit proceeded to tell them the story of a poet named Lotus who lived in the city back then. It told them how her husband had been framed and killed by a jealous noble, and how the event drove Lotus to release her anguish and heartbreak upon the public. Since that night, the rabbit said solemnly, the city sank under a frightful curse that continued to that very day.

The twins were silent. Then Yun whispered, "So the curse on the city is real?"

"Indubitably it's real." The Jade Rabbit cocked its head. *"I just told you that, didn't I? You need to listen better if you want to survive in this world."*

Yun stammered something in response; the attentive twelve-year-old wasn't used to being admonished like that. Mei elbowed her brother, biting back a smile. "Excuse me, Jade Rabbit," she said, having newfound immense respect for the creature. "What did you mean earlier when you said we have 'the gift'?"

"It's obvious. I was referring to your dreamweaving abilities. Why else are you here?"

Mei and Yun glanced at each other. The Jade Rabbit, sharp as it was, immediately caught the meaning of the quick exchange.

"*Hmm. I take it the jar of dreams you released is not yours?*"

"Jar of *dreams?*" repeated both twins.

"*Pardon me—jar of* nightmares," the rabbit corrected. "*The bulk of the dreamcloud's colors were bright green and black, which mean anger, uneasiness, fear. Ideally, you want dreams to be a soft blue, or bright yellow like sunshine.*"

The twins stared at each other. "We don't know anything about dreamweaving," Mei said to the rabbit. "Or what it even means."

"*Hmm.*" The Jade Rabbit seemed to ponder this for a few moments. "*A dreamweaver is someone who works with dreams—and nightmares. They have the power to control a dream, to affect it from all aspects, all angles . . . even from* within *the dream.*" The rabbit tilted its head and shrugged its shoulder. "*But never mind that. I must have misread you. Both of you give off the essence of a dreamweaver, and of this very city. I thought that was what attracted you here, in fact.*"

The twins must've looked confused, because the rabbit went on to explain. "*You have seen the residents here. They were, of course, not always in such a state. When the curse began, they suddenly found themselves cornered by their own nightmares: things they dread, suspicion of one another, despair. As the curse grew stronger each day, their reality became similar to a dreamlike state. And in a dream, time is boundless. People became trapped in time. The residents you encountered today—they're not ghosts. They're still alive, just not in* our *present.*"

Mei and Yun did not completely follow, but they shivered at the rabbit's words. They thought of the odd appearances of the people they'd met, how they were not quite natural. Pounding in the back of their minds was also the troubling question of why Grandpa owned a jar of dreams, and what else he might've kept from them.

"How was one poet able to do all this?" whispered Mei.

"What you need to understand is the physical world is rather like a mirror of the dream world. They work together in harmony, the same way the moon has, for you humans, a dark side and a bright side. In fact, the universe is made up of such contrary forces. They are an ancient magic, very powerful. You can find them everywhere in nature: winter and summer, chaos and order. They are inseparable, and neither side can exist without the other."

The idea sounded like one of those mystical concepts Elder Liu or Grandpa might talk about. "What do you mean 'neither side can exist without the other'?" asked Yun timidly, still embarrassed about the Jade Rabbit's earlier rebuke.

"Take the example of light and darkness," said the Jade Rabbit. *"Darkness exists because of the absence of light. And without darkness, one would not recognize light for what it is. Same with everything else. Seasons change. Life comes after death, and vice versa. Neither side is superior to the other, but a correct balance is essential. When there is proper balance, the world lives in harmony. And where there* isn't ..."

"You have the City of Ashes?" ventured Yun.

The Jade Rabbit nodded. *"Imbalance means disturbance. There is great power in such a disruption. Lotus was able to tap into this power. She was consumed by her anger and hate, both of which came from her wounded heart. The imbalance threw both her and this city into what they are now."*

71

There was a long silence as the twins digested the creature's words. "I never knew the physical world was linked to the dream world," Mei said, her skin prickling.

"Linked to it, yes, but not identical—the dream world isn't quite like the physical world," answered the Jade Rabbit. *"Your subconscious plays a big role in the dream world. In the physical world, you raise your arm to reach for an apple in a tree. In the dream world, the apple comes to you because it knows you want it. That's how it works for most people."*

"Most people?" echoed Mei.

"Dreamweavers, of course, are different. They can exert more control in such a scenario. They have the ability to affect the flow and outcome of dreams—their own, and others', if they so choose. How tall is the tree, how fast does the apple fall, its color and flavor. . . . The dream world is more malleable for a dreamweaver; it's a realm they can enter at any point they desire, provided they make their wishes clear before falling asleep."

"How many dreamweavers are out there?" asked Yun, thinking of Grandpa.

"Oh, they're relatively rare," the Jade Rabbit answered vaguely. *"Their magic is usually inherited or attained from a special source. . . ."* The creature looked the twins over once more and asked, *"Where in the physical world are you two from?"*

"A village just over the mountains," said Mei. She went on to describe the strange clouds that recently arrived there, the moon's disappearance, and the storms that followed. "Our grandpa is in trouble," she finished. "So is our village. A lot of other . . . weird things . . . have happened in the last few days."

The Jade Rabbit seemed to frown, if rabbits could frown.

"I know the place you speak of. It sounds like it's somehow been affected by the curse. Tell me, did anyone unusual visit your village in the past few days?"

"Just the emperor's son," Yun answered. "He came all the way from the Imperial City for the Mid-Autumn Festival."

The Jade Rabbit looked at the sky. *"Mm-hmm. That's quite an honor,"* was all it said.

Mei and Yun also looked up at the moonless sky.

"Do you really live on the moon?" whispered Mei.

"Yes. As I've stated, I am the Guardian of the Moon."

"Can you still get home if the moon is gone?"

"Of course. The moon is still visible in other areas. I simply travel to one of those places and return home by standing in the moonlight."

There were many more questions the twins wanted to ask the marvelous rabbit. But one question in particular burned in the back of their throats.

"You said the curse started seventy years ago," said Yun. "What about the people who traveled to the city afterward? How would they even get in?"

"Although the city is locked to the outside, every now and then, people manage to enter. Like you."

"Like our parents," whispered Mei. She instinctively touched the butterfly pin in her hair.

The Jade Rabbit looked at her questioningly. Yun explained, "Our parents came to this city six years ago to learn about what happened here."

"I see." The Jade Rabbit seemed to understand, without either twin saying so, how they'd never heard from their parents again. It dipped its head slightly, and its voice had a trace

of pity. *"If they really were able to get past these walls, then they're still here in this nebulous nightmare."*

"Alive?" demanded Mei.

"Presumably. Except everything to them is as it was six years ago. They would not know time has passed."

There was a long silence. It was broken by Yun. "How do we find them?" he asked shakily. "How do we rescue them?"

"Finding them may be difficult. There are several thousand people in this city, all trapped in time. Rescuing them is only possible if the curse is lifted."

"Can't you help? You can use your magical rabbit powers, can't you?"

At this, the Jade Rabbit stood straight, looking rather affronted. *"I cannot reverse this curse. It was brought about by misused magic and took on a life of its own. I am powerless to intervene at this point, and frankly, it's best that I stop getting involved in human affairs altogether."* It twitched its pink nose, seemingly trying to convince itself of this last point. *"I presented myself to you only because I was curious about your essence and wanted to know what drew you to this bleak place. But I have my answers, and I shall be going. . . ."*

"Wait!" pleaded Mei. "Please stay. You have to help us. We need to rescue our grandpa, too. We need to get to the emperor's palace in time, before it's too late."

"And that'll be impossible without horses or adults helping us," added Yun.

"I am sorry. I cannot undo this curse or help you."

The Jade Rabbit turned away and started to shimmer, as if to disappear. Desperate, Mei reached out and grabbed the rabbit's hind paw.

"Ouch!" Tears sprung to Mei's eyes as she whipped her hand back. Her fingers burned white hot.

The rabbit turned to face the twins again. It watched the tears fall down Mei's face. It studied Yun's quivering chin.

"There is one solution," it finally told them in a resigned voice. *"You could try appealing to Lotus—her ghost, her spirit. She unleashed the curse, and therefore she is the only one who can break it."*

"Where is she?" asked the twins.

The Jade Rabbit paused. *"In the Temple of Fire."*

CHAPTER ELEVEN

+—

The Temple of Fire

The stairway to the Temple of Fire had forty-four steps. By the time the twins reached the top, they could see over most of the rooftops in the city. It was brighter up there, the stars above unobstructed by buildings. Mei and Yun looked past the city walls where the mountains' majestic silhouettes were illuminated by the infinite stars.

Their breathtaking view was somewhat dampened by the presence of four hooded figures standing right behind them.

"It's okay, they can't see us," Mei whispered to Yun. "Remember what the Jade Rabbit said."

That didn't stop the siblings from walking stiffly—and holding their breaths—when they slipped past the guards.

"Lotus's followers," the Jade Rabbit had explained, when Yun asked the creature about the hooded figures. *"She had*

a good number of enemies after she set the curse over the city, but she also had a number of people who stood by her. This is true for everyone who finds themselves in a position of power, no matter how kind or cruel they are, in every dynasty."

According to the Jade Rabbit, the temple used to be a sacred home for a group of monks. Lotus took it over shortly after she cast the curse. She had a lot of magic inside her at that point, the rabbit said, and a temple was the ideal place to house such power. The people in the city renamed the building the Temple of Fire. The remaining residents who were brave enough tried to appeal to Lotus to end the curse.

"None have succeeded," the rabbit had concluded.

"Then how can you expect us to?" Yun had protested in reply.

"I never said I expect you to." The Jade Rabbit wiggled its cotton tail. *"In fact, I doubt you'll see her at all, since you've come seven decades too late. But I wish you luck nonetheless. I'm interested to hear how it goes. Lotus may still be angry with me after all these years...."*

Mei led the way into the temple. The floor beneath their boots was smooth and cold. Yun lit the gas lantern again. The flickering light showed they were in a round room, with another set of stairs ahead leading into the darkness.

"Up?" Mei said reluctantly.

Yun nodded. "Unfortunately, that's what the Jade Rabbit said."

Their footsteps echoed in the large chamber as they climbed the stairs. There was something terribly strange and foreboding about the temple—the enormous walls that seemingly stretched into nothing, the dark windows, the emptiness of it all. And with each step the twins took, it felt like they were getting closer to something they ought to stay far, far away from.

The end of the stairway led to a closed set of red doors. A large emblem of a flame was etched in the center, half on each door.

The Jade Rabbit had given them instructions to go through the doors. Mei and Yun glanced at each other, then pushed open one side. The door creaked forward heavily, weighing at least fifty pounds.

The door opened to a circular chamber. Mei and Yun gasped.

The room must have once been beautiful: enormous painted scrolls decorated the walls, and gilded molding bordered the ornate floor and ceiling. But many of the paintings had been ripped and punctured with ugly gashes, and the gold was tarnished brown. The dim chamber was lit by a dancing flame in the far corner, next to the only window in the room. The fire appeared to float in midair, as if suspended by an invisible torch. All the while, a musky odor hung over the chamber, like it hadn't been aired out in a long time. Two embroidered pillows lay against the wall.

Mei and Yun moved uneasily toward the fire. "Hello?" Mei whisper-called, afraid to disturb the still air. Yun didn't say anything at all, but started biting his nails again.

Then they noticed the thin wisps of smoke that drifted across the chamber. Thin colored threads weaved between them; every so often, the colors pulsated like a fainter version of the nightmare clouds in Grandpa's jar.

The twins glanced at each other. They waited for a few moments, then called out again. Nothing.

"The Jade Rabbit told us we may need to wait a while," Mei said, shifting her bag.

"A while could be days, or weeks," said Yun. He took out the leftover buns, and the twins ate as they waited. Yun's gaze once more fell on the pillows against the wall. "We might as well rest for the night. It's been a long day."

"*Aiyah*," groaned Mei. The last place she wanted to fall asleep was there, inside a building called the Temple of Fire, with a vengeful spirit prowling the premises.

"Well, I don't mind," said Yun. "Sleeping comes naturally to me, I can do it with my eyes closed."

He headed over to the pillows. Each one was made of fine red silk and had intricate silver patterns under a fine layer of dust. He carefully laid down his bag and lantern, then laid his head upon one of the pillows.

It was the most comfortable pillow he'd ever used. "I'll just rest my eyes for a few minutes," he called. Even mid-sentence, he could feel his voice getting slower, and his eyes felt heavier. The long day's journey had sunk into his body, and there didn't seem to be anything better in the whole world than falling asleep. "This is nicer than our beds back home," he yawned.

Mei stared horrified at her brother across the room. But after a few moments, fatigue overwhelmed her, and she finally gave in and did the same.

"I swear, Yun, if we get killed in here, it's your fault...." She pressed her head against the soft pillow, willing her eyes to stay open. "We ought to stay awake," she murmured. "We don't know what's lurking around the..."

Within minutes, both siblings were fast asleep.

✳

They didn't know how long they'd been sleeping, only that a rumble shook the floor, and they found themselves jolting awake in the chamber. Only the chamber no longer looked the way it did when they'd entered. It was bright inside, as if sunlight had flooded in and filled every corner—yet that was impossible because the sky outside the small circular window was dark. The light bounced off the gilded floor and ceiling, which had been miraculously polished new. The paintings had also been restored. Not only that, but the scenes on the scrolls were *alive;* the trees had leaves that swayed and the streams had liquid that flowed. Flocks of geese flew on the paper from east to west. The twins stared mesmerized at the moving pictures.

"Your inquiry?" said a voice to their left.

They turned to see a tall, stately woman on the other side of the chamber, beneath a painting of blossom trees. She wore a slim white-and-pink stitched tunic and a matching skirt that draped behind her. Her long hair gleamed black, and her attractive face lent her a kind demeanor, even though she did not smile. She looked no older than twenty.

"Inquiry?" she repeated.

Mei was the first to come to her senses. "We're here to see Lotus," she spoke up.

"I am she."

"Oh! So then...*you* were the one who set the...the terrible curse upon the city...." Mei trailed off as Lotus stared evenly at her. She elbowed her brother for help.

Yun had been gaping at Lotus. He turned beet red, then

mumbled, "We're, um, here to speak to you. But first, what is this place?"

"This is my dream chamber. Isn't it lovely?"

The twins nodded, mostly because they didn't dare upset the person who had set a curse on an entire city.

"What's a dream chamber?" Mei asked. "Are you a—a dreamweaver?"

"I don't know what that is," Lotus answered calmly as she began approaching the twins. "My dream chamber is simply a place where I dwell to pass the time. Visitors come now and then to ask me things. So let's get this over with. Who are you and what do you want?"

After the twins politely stammered quick introductions, Yun explained how the Jade Rabbit had told them about Lotus, and how their mother and father had come to the city six years ago and hadn't returned to their village.

"We're hoping you can, er, lift the curse," he finished weakly.

Lotus raised her chin slightly. She pressed her red lips together into a thin line. "How interesting," she said airily.

The twins waited as Lotus turned to examine the scroll painting behind her. The woman touched the ink, the fluttering pink blossom trees.

"My son lost his mother and father, too," she said, still facing away from the twins. "His father was executed for a crime he didn't commit. And his mother was swallowed by a horrible magic. Magic given to her by the wretched Jade Rabbit."

Mei and Yun shared a sidelong glance. "Um, you're talking about yourself, right?" clarified Yun.

Lotus turned around, her eyes focused on something in the

distance, past the twins. "Tell me, then," she continued as if Yun had not interrupted. "Why should I grant you your wish, when multiple other people have suffered similar tragedies?"

Mei piped up. "Because it's awful?"

Yun cringed—he could hear the bold defiance creeping into his sister's tone—and quickly added, "It *is* awful what happened to your son, but that was seventy years ago, right? He's lived a full life by now. Whereas Mei and I, you see, we're both twelve. We have our whole lives ahead of us."

Lotus's eyes flashed dangerously, and Yun abruptly fell silent.

"My son was very young at the time," Lotus replied. "He had his whole life ahead of him, too. But the Jade Rabbit stole him from me."

The woman moved closer to the twins, who backed up against the wall. Lotus leaned in; her long fingers closed around Yun's wrist, and her face hovered just above Yun's ear. Her lips curved into a smile. If a stranger had chanced upon the scene, they might've thought the woman was a doting mother or aunt telling the boy a secret.

"Do not lecture *me* about time," Lotus said in a soft voice. "For me, time stopped long ago." She leaned back and released the vice grip around Yun's wrist. They left white imprints in his skin. "Deluded is the person who thinks their own story is more important than everyone else's. Deluded and selfish. Many people have come to me, pleading for me to stop the curse. 'I miss my family,' they say. Or 'I want the city to be safe again.' Yet when I pleaded the dastardly Noble General to spare my husband, did I get my wish?"

With her back straight and her chin high, Lotus stepped

back. Even when angry, she was quite beautiful. But looks were deceiving, as Mei and Yun had already realized. Lotus did not look like someone who'd doom an entire city to seventy years' of misfortune and waste, yet there she was.

"Why didn't you go after the Noble General?" asked Yun, remembering what the Jade Rabbit had said about the high-ranking official who caused Lotus so much grief. "He's the one who recommended that the emperor build the wall around the city, wasn't he?"

"Yes, he was." Lotus's voice tightened. "I tried to go after him, but my magic prevents me from leaving this city. It locks me in, more than silly walls ever could."

"How?" asked Yun, who couldn't help being inquisitive, even in the presence of one so powerful.

"I don't understand the details. You mustn't ask me. You'd have to ask the one who granted me these powers. But never mind that. At least the Noble General and his descendants know enough to never set foot here. My spell would not serve them well if they tried."

"Can't you let us see our parents, at least?" Yun begged.

"Certainly not. I grant no special favors to anyone."

"Well, if you won't do that, and you won't lift the curse, can you at least help us get to the Imperial City?" said Mei, who was getting angry, too. "Our grandpa's been wrongly arrested—you know how that's like, don't you? We need to get to the emperor's palace. Your curse basically made the entire city deserted, so no one else can help us."

"Our village has been buried in snow," added Yun. "All the crops and animals died. We'll all be in for a long, miserable winter."

"Also caused by your curse," Mei pointed out.

Lotus studied the twins with an odd expression on her face. "That is not possible," she finally said. "My power is confined to this city alone."

"Well, obviously it *isn't*."

Lotus's mouth pursed from side to side, as if words were fighting to get out. Then she spoke:

"A river flows downstream
And joins the glittering sea.
A human flows downstream
And remains dust forever."

The poet strode toward the other side of the chamber, where she studied the blossom trees again.

"When my husband was alive, I'd recite my poetry to him," she said quietly. "He wasn't the strongest reader— spelling and grammar rules often confused him—so he memorized the poems and recited them. We'd spend hours under the blossom trees together, speaking poetry."

She laid a finger on the scroll and slowly traced the trees once more.

"The curse controls me as much as it controls the others," she continued. "It is surprisingly easy to destroy something with mere words." After several long moments, she looked over her shoulder at the twins. "It is time to awaken you two. I cannot help you."

Yun racked his brains. "What if we told you we can clear your husband's name?" he said. "Then would you help us?"

Lotus's back stiffened. She turned to face Yun slowly, the

trace of an amused smile on her face. "How would you do this?" she asked.

"We'll tell the emperor," Yun lied. "Our grandpa was wrongly arrested, too."

Beside him, Mei held her breath.

"You say you're going to the Imperial City to prove your grandfather's innocence?" said Lotus after a pause.

"Yes."

"And therefore, you *think* you know the anguish I feel."

"Oh, definitely," Mei and Yun echoed quickly.

"Unfortunately, there is no sense anymore in trying to prove my husband's innocence. The wicked Noble General has ties to the imperial bloodline. He has the emperor under his influence, and he isn't going to let a couple of"—here Lotus swept her eyes over the twins and frowned slightly—"*kids* prove him wrong. You'd have no luck."

"The Noble General is surely already dead," pointed out Yun, who had been thinking about the timeline and calculating how long ago this all had happened.

Lotus considered this. "Yes, I suppose time passes differently in the outside world. You mentioned the curse has lasted for seventy years? The Noble General, old as he was when I knew him, is at least one hundred nowadays, if he still breathes." Her eyes darkened. "A quiet death is too good for him."

The paintings around the room began to shake, as if rattled by an earthquake. The room's light began to glow hazy. Then, as quickly as it started, everything became still.

Lotus brushed a loose strand of hair from her face. "Perhaps I should settle for the next best thing, now that he's no longer controlling things from up in the Imperial Palace."

The twins waited with bated breath.

"Very well. Prove my husband was also innocent while you're at the palace. If you somehow demonstrate that he was framed by the ignoble general ... if you clear his name, for all of China to hear ... then, and only then, will I lift the curse."

"Right then," said Yun hesitantly, "but like we said, we need help getting to the Imperial City. It's over a month's journey by foot, and—"

"My dear boy," said Lotus without any trace of warmth, "I already said I cannot help you with that. I am bound here. Besides, you've already met someone who can assist you." She waited for the children to answer. When they only stared at her in confusion, she said impatiently, "The Jade Rabbit."

"The Jade Rabbit wouldn't help us—" Mei began.

"That was before it knew of our deal," Lotus interrupted. "I promise to lift the curse if your end of the deal is fulfilled. Under these new conditions, that harebrained creature will be happy to aid you."

Mei and Yun looked at each other. They didn't seem to have another choice.

"All right," said Yun. "It's a deal. If we clear your husband's name ..."

"... then you will release the city—and our parents—from the curse," finished Mei.

"Fine, fine. Farewell, then, until we meet again." Lotus smiled and clapped once. The light in the chamber faded to black.

The next moment, Mei and Yun found themselves lying on their pillows, the empty chamber restored to its original desolate state.

CHAPTER TWELVE

十二

Voyage Through the Sky

The Jade Rabbit was waiting for the twins outside the temple. The rabbit read the troubled expressions on their faces, and began kindly, *"Do not fret. It has been ages, and the temple has remained empty for—"*

"No, it wasn't empty, we saw her!" the twins shouted.

"Ah...well, many have tried before you, and none could convince her—"

"No, no, she agreed!"

The twins explained feverishly how Lotus would lift the curse, restoring the city and allowing them to see their parents, only if they proved her husband's innocence. The Jade Rabbit listened quietly, its ears straight. When Mei and Yun finished, the rabbit murmured, *"Hmm, this is a development."*

"She said you'd help us get to the Imperial City," Yun said

nervously. "But—but I know you said you wouldn't use your magic to help humans anymore."

The Jade Rabbit twitched its whiskers. There was a long pause.

"I did not ask you children earlier," it said quietly. *"Tell me, where did you obtain your jar of dreams?"*

"It was our grandpa's jar," answered Mei. "We found it in the kitchen."

"Ah." The answer seemed to make up the Jade Rabbit's mind. Something glinted in its eyes. *"Yes, I will help you get to the Imperial City. If the emperor's son left your village little more than two days ago, then he won't arrive at the palace for seven more days, at least. You will use this extra time to do what you can to prove Lotus's husband's innocence."*

The twins exchanged a glance. They were suddenly feeling very unsure about the deal they'd made with Lotus. Going to the city to ask to see the emperor was one thing. Trying to prove someone's innocence to undo a seventy-year-old curse was a whole other issue. They didn't even know where to start.

"I suppose we can try going through the history scrolls at the palace library," Yun said, his voice faltering. "Baba always talked about it being a treasure trove of every single thing recorded in China. They don't just let anybody in, though."

"We'll have to break in, then," Mei said slowly. "If it's a treasure trove of records, they'll have records of executions along with everything else."

"But if we get caught, we'll be jailed and executed ourselves."

"Or worse," chimed in the Jade Rabbit conversationally.

"It will indeed be dangerous, but I believe you children are uniquely equipped for this task."

The rabbit saw the looks on their faces and told them, "Throughout history, there have always been people who were not deterred by fear of punishment, because a greater purpose called. Follow the greater purpose."

It held up its paws and conjured a pool of bright white light—moonlight, it looked like. The glow surrounded the three of them. The next thing Mei and Yun knew, they felt weightless, and were being lifted slowly into the air like floating lanterns.

Up and up they went, higher and higher, until their feet were in line with the city's rooftops. Yun flailed his arms, muttering under his breath, "This is not good, this is *not* good." Mei, meanwhile, laughed and shouted, "This is better than climbing trees!"

They rose past a drifting cloud. The twins felt their weight return, and their bodies bounded downward. Before either of them could release a scream, the cloud moved beneath them, and their feet landed on the soft white puff. They stood in the sky, breathless and stunned.

"This cloud will take you straight to the Imperial City," the Jade Rabbit said. "You'll arrive in a day. The cloud will protect you from the elements—heat, cold, rain, even snow, though I do not believe you'll encounter any."

Yun and Mei patted the cloud. Its delicate white wisps brushed against their skin.

"This isn't a dream, right?" sputtered Yun, rubbing his eyes.

"No, it is not a dreamcloud," replied the Jade Rabbit. "It

is simply a cloud of the sky, with a little additional magic from the moon."

"No, I meant, am I dreaming?"

"You're as awake as I am. And now, I wish you well. Remember, a journey of a thousand miles begins with a single step." The Jade Rabbit suddenly extended its front paws and gently held Yun's hand, then Mei's. It pressed its tiny nose against their fingers. "It has been wonderful meeting you children."

The realization that the Jade Rabbit was leaving them jolted a series of questions from each twin.

"Wait!" said Mei. "Can you tell us more about—about dreamweaving—"

"—and Lotus's husband's crime—" added Yun.

"—and our parents?"

"Patience is a virtue. At the moment, all these questions are extra baggage. You shall discover the truth of all these matters soon enough, but for now, focus on your primary task." The rabbit gave them a small nod. "Good luck. I sensed greatness in you the moment we met."

With that, the Jade Rabbit disappeared in a shimmer of white. The cloud began carrying the twins away from the City of Ashes.

·✳·

Most birds, if you ask them in a way that you both understand each other, will agree that flying is an exhilarating experience, and they cannot understand how humans and other creatures put up with moving about so slowly. As the cloud carried Mei and Yun across the sky with surprising speed, as the wind whipped their hair back and the stars twinkled overhead, the twins began wondering the same thing.

"I'll never walk again!" Mei shouted above the wind. There was something extraordinary about being on top of the world, and seeing the distant cities and hidden villages sprawled on all sides. A small part of her had always longed to travel to new places. Just like her parents had.

She gripped the cloud and leaned over the edge to watch the trees, rivers, and mountains pass by. It was just like the tales of the fabled Monkey King and his magic cloud, which he used to traverse the skies. From the cloud's height, only the highest mountain peaks loomed over them, large impressive cliffs of bare rock with sprouts of vegetation along the top. The cloud navigated around these hazards expertly.

"You'll still have to walk after this is over," Yun replied. He sat in the very middle of the cloud, with his legs curled tightly under his arms. His face was somewhat green.

"Just close your eyes and go to sleep," Mei called back, exasperated. "I'll let you know when we arrive."

As the cloud flew through the night, dawn broke on the horizon. The sky grew pink, then orange, then pale blue. The trees, waters, and mountains slowly regained their colors. Because the Imperial City lay to the north, the already cold air got even colder the farther they went. But the Jade Rabbit had been correct in that the cloud offered ample protection. It stayed toasty warm beneath the twins' bodies, as if it had soaked up all the sun's rays, and the two siblings could stretch parts of it over themselves like a heavy blanket. They sat against the cloud, drifting past large, green fields of rice paddies, watching the red-and-orange tinged trees of the north roll into view, floating past the occasional flock of geese heading south for the winter.

By noon, their exhilaration wore off. They ate a quick lunch of leftover buns, then finally dozed for several hours (they'd only slept a wink the night before, after all). Around mid-afternoon, as they were flying over a seemingly endless range of brown mountains with snow-capped peaks that extended even higher than the mountains back home, they began discussing Grandpa's mysterious jar.

"Do you think Grandpa was a dreamweaver, then?" Mei guessed.

Yun looked down at his bag, which still held their grandfather's prized possession. He nodded.

"So I was right about him using magic," Mei said triumphantly. "It wasn't *just* a metaphor."

"Okay, yes, you were right," said Yun. "But it raises a plethora of questions." He squinted, shielding his eyes from the sunlight that gleamed off the snowcaps. "Question one: Why did Grandpa keep this secret from us? Question two: Why was he collecting nightmares? Question three: Did our parents have this ability?"

Mei rummaged in Yun's bag and took out the porcelain jar. Most the contents inside had leaked out in the City of Ashes, but there was still a puff of flashing green-and-black clouds left at the very bottom. She thought of the colored mists they saw growing up in the village—mists that their mother had seen, too. That explained one thing, at least.

"Mama saw the dreams like we did," she said quietly. "Maybe that's one of the reasons she and Baba were drawn to the City of Ashes. Maybe she was attracted by its 'essence,' as the Jade Rabbit said."

"Maybe," Yun repeated doubtfully. He liked to avoid jumping to conclusions until he had every piece of factual evidence assembled in front of him. "Dreamweaving aside, that's odd the curse spilled over to our village, isn't it? Lotus seems to think it's confined within the premises."

"Lotus seems to have no clue what's happening outside her city," Mei snorted derisively. "All she knows is her grudge against the Noble General."

Yun, deep in concentration, didn't respond for a few moments. "The Jade Rabbit asked if anyone unusual visited our village," he said finally, with his eyes closed.

"Yes, I know," said Mei. "And we said the emperor's son had."

"Don't you see, Mei?" Yun said, his eyes now open and widening in excitement. "Anyone traveling from the Imperial City to our village would have to pass by the City of Ashes on their way!"

"You're saying *the emperor's son* set off the curse?"

"Yes, or someone in his entourage! That must be why the Jade Rabbit asked us about it. Somehow, his passing by must have brought the curse to our village, like water spilling from an overflowing pot."

Mei raised her eyebrow. "I *thought* he was kind of weird," she remarked. "Remember how he was speaking in riddles toward the end of the night?"

"That might've been because of Lotus's magic, too," answered Yun. "I don't know."

"Great, so we know Lotus hates him for some reason,

too," said Mei flatly. "Who else does she hate? Our parents? They didn't even do anything to her."

"Well..." Yun tried to keep his voice steady. "At least now we know why they never returned."

After a somber silence, they decided to focus on the task at hand. They began to plan out what they'd do once they reached the palace. Somehow, they would need to navigate the imperial court undetected. The twins tried to rack their memories of all the things their father had told them about life in the Imperial City. They thought of his anecdotes about stern officials and joking guards, about royal children who sometimes got up to mischief. He'd told them how at the palace, poor scholars were afforded privileges that they could never have dreamed of elsewhere.

Out of all of Baba's tales, their favorite was actually the story of how he left the palace life: of the spring he'd traveled south to research the villages around the Pearl River, and how he'd met Mama one night by the river, under the moonlight. He had known right then and there that he wouldn't be returning to the Imperial City.

"We'll have to disguise ourselves as servants," decided Mei, recalling Baba's descriptions of the hundreds upon hundreds of attendants and laborers who kept the palace running and the emperor happy. "Blend in with the people at the palace, maybe pick up some information that way. We'll have to avoid any sharp-looking officials, though."

"Agreed," said Yun. "And like I said before, we should try the Imperial Library. It's our best bet for finding more information about Lotus's husband and his trial."

"It might actually be doable," said Mei, lying back on the cloud.

"Yes," Yun agreed, in spite of himself.

The twins felt calm. Their earlier worries had evaporated. Now that they'd been exposed to the exhilarating ride, now that they knew the Jade Rabbit was on their side (even if the creature didn't officially say so), now that they had a plan, they felt a renewed surge of confidence.

That's the funny thing about confidence. Your situation, if you look at it, is oftentimes the exact same as before. The only things that have really changed are your own thoughts on the matter.

✳

By dusk, the capital came into view.

The large rectangular palace complex within the city looked impressive even from a distance, enclosed by four red walls and a moat. It was at least five times larger than their village, and appeared bigger even than the City of Ashes. The cloud slowed and lowered. The twins peeked over the edge at the neat rows of yellow roofs and numerous complexes outlined inside the walls. They floated past the main southern gate, which was flanked by guards.

"That's a lot of space for the emperor to live in," called Mei above the wind.

"But it's not just the emperor who lives there," Yun called back. "He's got officials, guards, servants, and his entire family."

"I know that, but even so, there's probably more space

than is needed by all those people. This could fit our village *ten* times over."

"If you ruled the land, you'd want to live in an enormous fortress, too. To stay safe from your enemies and all." Yun pointed to a cluster of buildings near the entrance that had black rooftops. "There's the Imperial Library!" Even with his poor eyesight, he could see how the structure stood out in the midst of yellow-gold roofs. "Baba said it's the only building whose roof is painted black. Fireproof, so it protects the scrolls and books inside against flames."

Two giant bronze statues stood on either side of the marble stairs to the pavilion: a dragon and a phoenix, both mid-flight. Yun said he'd once read about art symbolism in some of Baba's scrolls. "The emperor is usually represented by a dragon," he explained, "and the empress is represented by a phoenix."

"We can admire the art some other time, Yun," Mei said. "Right now we have a job to do. Okay, cloud. Stop!"

The cloud kept drifting.

"Stop!" repeated Mei, stamping on the cloud.

The twins took turns shouting instructions at the cloud. It stopped moving just above a large slanted rooftop in the middle of the city. It lowered itself toward the roof, farther and farther, until Mei and Yun were just a jump away. This must be their cue.

Clutching their bags, they hoisted themselves over the cloud and landed on the golden rooftop. As soon as their feet touched the log-like tiles, they found themselves sliding dangerously down the slanted edge. Even Mei, who had climbed numerous trees with ease, had trouble keeping her footing on the slippery slope. Yun yelled as he lost his balance.

Mei's lightning-fast reflexes kicked in, and she grabbed a carved golden phoenix that adorned the ridge with one hand and gripped her brother's hand with the other. They climbed back onto the tiles and tried to regain their stability.

"This is impossible to climb," gasped Mei.

"Probably to prevent infiltrators like us from getting up here," answered Yun. "Clever architecture, if you think about it."

They carefully slid from the top roof to a secondary one below. Once there, they leapt toward the smooth platform and landed with a *thump*. After stopping to catch their breath, they looked back at the enormous building they'd jumped from.

They stood before a regal red structure, with columns as big as trees stretching in both directions. The twins were reminded of the Temple of Fire, except this building did not have an austere, abandoned appearance. Rather, it looked warm and inviting, though there was no doubt it served an important purpose. Soft light shone from behind the checkered-patterned windows. Running parallel underneath the slippery roof were wooden beams decorated with sweeping paintings of gold and teal dragons. The twins glanced at each other. A gleaming place such as this must be reserved for none other than . . .

"The emperor is waiting!" called a pair of voices behind them.

The twins turned to see two harried men in long gray robes and blue jackets running up the staircase. Mei and Yun jumped behind one of the columns just in time. With racing pulses, they watched the men disappear inside through the open doors.

"Now what?" Yun whispered. Now that the siblings were off the magic cloud and actually in the midst of things, they felt their fears about their task returning. "Blending in is all well and good, but how—"

Before Yun could continue, another voice spoke. A kid's voice. The twins slowly turned to the source and found themselves staring at a small boy hanging from the top of the pillar. The boy wore expensive-looking silk robes and a smug grin. He dangled both their bags in his hand.

"Well, well," he called down. "You're either thieves or beggars. Whom should I alert?"

The boy jumped to the ground with effortless nimbleness. He was no larger than Mei or Yun. His hair was knotted in a small bun on top of his head. In his left hand he carried a pointy bamboo stick, the tip of which was sharp enough to impale someone. He held up the weapon menacingly while proudly telling the twins that he'd whittled it himself.

"That's great," Mei said with forced enthusiasm. She figured the longer she and Yun stalled the boy, the likelier it was that they could escape. "My brother and I—we love dueling with swords."

"With real swords?" said the boy with a raised eyebrow.

"Oh, yes. We've been dueling since we were little."

The boy narrowed his eyes. "Prove it. You look like nothing more than a pair of peasants."

"We're expert sword fighters," Mei said, trying not to feel the sting of the boy's comment. "We left our weapons at home, unfortunately. We'll go get them, then meet you back here, okay? Can we get our bags back?"

The boy sliced the air with the bamboo stick several

times. "What do you take me for, a baby with an ox's brain?" he mocked.

"Oxen are quite clever, and their brains would be too big to fit inside an infant's head," Yun said matter-of-factly.

The boy stabbed the stick into one of the bags, ripping the fabric. Yun lunged for the bag. *Whoosh!* The bamboo stick swung dangerously close to his face, and he jumped back in alarm.

"Look, we'll prove who we are," pleaded Mei. "Just give us back our stuff, and—"

Rapid footsteps sounded behind them. Another man in a gray robe and blue jacket was there. The twins realized the outfit must have been the dress code of the palace servants and made a mental note for later. The man ran up to the boy and said urgently, "Move along, we need to get you dressed for the banquet."

"Shuffle off and choke on a fishbone," the boy snapped. "I'm busy."

Mei and Yun were speechless. Never had they ever spoken to an adult like that, not even to Madam Hu. If a child talked like that to an elder back at the village, he or she would get whacked with a cane.

The man, however, didn't seem fazed. "Forgive me, Master Fu-Fu," he replied with a slight bow. (Mei and Yun gawked at each other—*master?*) "But the banquet starts in an hour. The emperor requires your presence."

"I don't want to see Uncle. He has plenty of other people to keep him company."

The servant seemed exasperated. His head bobbed from side to side, as if searching for a solution to pop out of the air. That was when he noticed Mei and Yun more closely.

"Are you two new?" he said suspiciously. "You're not from the maids' quarters, are you?"

"Yes!" Mei said, just as Yun sputtered, "No."

Fu-Fu smirked. "They're with me." He pointed the sharp bamboo stick at Yun. "The boy is supposed to clean my chamber pot later. The girl can clean my room."

Before either Mei or Yun could protest this arrangement, one of the men who had passed by earlier joined them. He had a pointy face and a mustache and beard, and was a head taller than the other man, though that partly may have been due to his unusually long neck. His demeanor reminded the twins of an angry crane.

"Don't just stand there like a lump!" the crane-like man barked at his companion. "The chefs need help preparing the pickled vegetables!" He turned to the twins and demanded, "Aren't you supposed to be at your assigned posts?"

"They are with Master Fu-Fu," the other man replied with a slight bow.

The first man spread his arms in exasperation, looking more crane-like than ever. "Fu-Fu, I've told you the servants are not your personal playmates," he said sternly.

"Fine," the boy grumbled. He pointed the sharp end of his stick at Mei. "You can let her go. But the other one has to fetch my dinner."

"Fine, fine. Go, take him!"

In one fluid movement, the crane's companion grabbed Yun's hand and escorted him inside the hall. The crane-like man watched them leave with a shake of his head, then turned to Mei and ordered, "Get back to the maids' quarters.

The empress's fourth daughter is waiting for someone to sew her robes." He added to Fu-Fu, "And you, go get dressed!"

The man must have had higher authority than the first servant, because Fu-Fu didn't argue with him. As he turned to leave, he asked, "Can these—uh, servants—be in the children's show later this week?" He smiled innocently. "They're *great* actors."

"Yes, yes, that can be arranged," the man replied dismissively.

And just like that, the twins were shepherded in opposite directions in the vast Imperial City.

CHAPTER THIRTEEN

十三

Chefs and Chopsticks

The sounds of sizzling pans and pounding knives greeted Yun as he followed the servant into the palace kitchen. His jaw dropped when he saw the size of the space. At least fifty people were scurrying around the large room, to and fro, chopping vegetables and mixing soups, fanning the wooden stoves, handling elaborate-looking porcelain platters, and carrying woks the size of the twins' entire table back home. The aromas from the foods would've normally made Yun's mouth water, but his stomach was filled with such dread that he probably couldn't have swallowed anything. All he wanted to do was curl in a corner.

Someone whipped an apron at him. He hastily put it on, then stepped beside a nearby chef who was slapping a large dead fish back and forth.

"You have to smack the seawater out of them!" the chef boomed. The chef had a round, strong body and pink cheeks. He looked like someone who'd grown up eating plenty of meat. The chef examined Yun with a raised eyebrow. "You're a bit young to be cooking. You some new chef-in-training?"

"Kind of," said Yun. "My, um, grandpa loves to cook."

The chef aimed a blow at the fish's head. Bits of fish grime sprayed Yun's cheek.

"Stop chewing your fingernails! No disgusting habits are allowed in my kitchen. I'll smack the seawater out of you too, you hear?" the chef roared again.

"Y-Yes, sir," Yun stammered, wiping the wet pieces from his face.

The chef threw the fish on a plate and bowed. "The name's Chef Fan."

Yun politely returned the bow. "I'm Yun," he said, realizing too late that he probably should've used a fake name.

"This kitchen's not for the weak, you hear? You have to show the food who's boss. Anything can be made into a delectable dish. Give me the hardest things to work with—quail eggs, crab legs, water chestnuts." Yun must have looked worried, because the chef said encouragingly, "Don't worry, practice makes perfect. Once you do something once, it becomes much easier the second time, and easier still the third."

Over the next hour, Chef Fan taught Yun how to gut a fish, how to pickle cucumbers, and how to test if a pot of water was hot enough. ("When you put your hand in and say 'Ouch,' then it's perfect, you hear?")

As odd and boisterous as Chef Fan was, there was no

denying he was a master at his craft. He had Yun taste-test his duck soup with yam.

"This is incredible," gasped Yun, who rarely said this about anyone's cooking besides Grandpa's. He tried to take a few more spoonfuls of the rich broth, but the chef whipped the bowl away.

"Of course it's incredible," Chef Fan said proudly. "Every dish I make is, you hear? Know why? I put my secret ingredient in each of them."

"What's the secret ingredient?" asked Yun.

Chef Fan looked around with what seemed like exaggerated shiftiness. He motioned for Yun to come closer. Yun leaned in.

"The secret ingredient . . ." breathed Chef Fan.

Yun listened closely.

". . . is NO LONGER A SECRET IF I TELL YOU, IS IT?" the chef roared into his ear.

Afterward, his ear still ringing, Yun followed the chef to the adjoining room, which was much quieter and less chaotic. Whistling teapots in different colors steamed from each side. The air bloomed with the earthy aroma from all kinds of teas—green tea, jasmine tea, chrysanthemum tea, black tea, ginger tea. Several people were carefully measuring tea leaves and herbs in little spoons.

"Great place to visit if you're sick," Chef Fan said. He fanned out his collar and added, "But stuffy and hot."

Yun agreed. Already, he could feel the sweat from the steam forming on his brows. He also felt drowsy from all the different scents. A long nap would be nice right about then.

Chef Fan spent several moments examining a jar of spices.

As he explained the different types of spices and which parts of the body they affected, a squawking noise startled Yun.

"Did you hear that?" he said.

"Yes, ginger is good for the throat, you hear?" the chef repeated louder.

"No, I heard a noise . . ."

"*Squaw-aw-awk.*"

"There it is again!" shouted Yun, bolting upright. His startled yell made the others in the room give him a dirty look.

Chef Fan's face darkened. "Oh, it's just Bendan." He reached into his coat with a grimace. The next moment, he held a small red-and-yellow parrot in his hand.

The parrot squawked. "*Just Bendan. Squawk.*"

"It can talk!" gasped Yun. Then, slightly embarrassed, he quickly corrected his mistake, "I meant it can mimic the sound of words. I don't believe parrots can actually communicate the way humans do. It's—"

"*Squawk! Communicate! Squawk!*"

"He's an idiot, is what this bird is!" Chef Fan boomed, going red in the face. "I have to keep him stuffed in my clothes. Otherwise, he causes—no, Bendan, stop!"

Bendan had flown to the other side of the room and was now circling a servant who held a tray of tea. "*An idiot, squawk! No, Bendan, stop! Squawk!*" Startled, the man dropped the tray with a loud clatter.

Chef Fan hurried after the bird, whistling and calling, "Come back here, Bendan, come back!"

The others in the room rolled their eyes and grumbled under their breaths. Apparently, this scene was nothing new. The parrot weaved through the crowd, then rose out of reach.

He dove toward an open teapot, presumably to hide inside. A nearby servant pulled it away at the last second, spilling hot liquid everywhere. There was a clamor of angry cries. Teacups shattered. Unattended teapots rattled as their water reached a boil, and the room reverberated with the shrill scream of their whistles. The bird shot off in search of a new target, nipped the hair of one servant, squawked in a laughing manner, then disappeared into one of the shelves.

"Emperor's breath smells, squawk! Like black fungi, squawk squawk!"

Chef Fan's face went from dark red to white. A servant nearby shot the chef an angry look and hissed, "Tell your silly bird to stop saying those things at once! Do you want us imprisoned for treason?"

"I'm trying to stop him! Here, Bendan, here!"

Two broken teacups and another chase around the room later, the pointy-faced man with the long neck from earlier stomped into the room. "Chef Fan!" he shouted above the commotion.

The room suddenly fell silent.

"Yes, sir?" squeaked the chef.

"If I see that idiotic bird loose one more time, you're going to have to fry it and feed it to the stray cats outside!"

Chef Fan managed to grab Bendan from the window and stuffed him in his pocket. He gave a shaky bow. "It won't happen again, sir."

After things settled down, Chef Fan wiped his shiny forehead. He motioned for Yun to follow him out to the quiet hallway. There, Chef Fan paced and muttered for several moments, kicking imaginary things, before heaving a sigh.

"This bird has given me more trouble than deboning a

chicken," he said. "He's gotten me into hot water multiple times—literally!"

"Why not get rid of him?" suggested Yun. He quickly added, "Not fry him, but release him into the wild?"

Chef Fan winced. "No can do. He belonged to my littlest girl, you hear?" Chef Fan gently took out the parrot again and stroked the bird's tiny red head. His voice fell. "She died of a fever a few months ago, and before she died, I promised her I'd always take care of her bird."

Yun understood. He and Mei had always felt protective of Smelly Tail because she had been their mother's cat. "What was that part about the emperor having fungi breath?" he asked.

"Just a harmless joke," Chef Fan chuckled. "He eats lots of mushrooms. Some of the other chefs and I were kidding around last night...stupid bird repeated it for all to hear. Shouldn't have brought him, but where else can I take him?"

"Can't you leave him in your quarters while you work?"

"No, because stupid Bendan here has offended enough people to get him killed in two seconds if I ever left him alone."

"Hmm, that's a dilemma," agreed Yun. He tried to come up with a solution. But none seemed to work. As Chef Fan explained, Bendan hated cages, hated the gardens outdoors, and had too many enemies watching him to be placed in a pet sitter's hands. Short of giving the parrot away, Yun didn't see how Chef Fan could solve his bird problem.

"Nah, I'll just have to cope with it," sighed the chef. "Cope and stay positive, you hear? It's hard, no doubt about it. My knees aren't as good as they used to be. And my aching back, it feels like a tiger is trying to claw its way out."

Doctor Po had always been good at curing the creaky

bones of the older villagers. He'd prescribe special ointments and correctly identify the muscle joints that needed treatment. Yun's heart sank when he thought of the doctor. How was the village faring? Was everyone still buried in snow? How was his grandpa? He needed to find Mei.

"You must think I'm a puny excuse of a chef, eh?" The chef slapped Yun's shoulder with a roaring laugh, jolting him from his thoughts. "Cheer up! Sometimes it's better to be a salamander than to be a babbling commander, you hear? Come, you act as if someone you knew has been kidnapped and taken on a long ride through the mountains."

"That's not a far-off statement," Yun murmured.

The chef cracked his knuckles and motioned for Yun to follow him back to the kitchen. "Watch, I'll show you how to prepare braised pork. Have you ever smacked a pig snout?"

✳

On the other side of the palace complex, Mei stood as still as stone in the quarters of the emperor's fourth daughter. She didn't move a muscle, not even when the heavy cloud of perfume in the air made her want to gag. There were thirty sharp pins clamped between her lips, and she did *not* want to accidentally swallow any.

Now thirty-one pins. The maid next to her had placed another one in Mei's mouth. The new pin pricked her tongue, but Mei forced herself to remain still.

"You are being very helpful, darling," the maid sang. With one pudgy hand, she held a spool of blue thread. With the other, she stretched out the right sleeve of the silk robe worn by the princess, who was sitting cross-legged on the bed.

"I don't remember seeing her before," the princess said with a skeptical glance at Mei.

"Now, now, Your Highness, goodness knows how big the Imperial Palace is, what with all the royal family members and officials and servants and military officers and..." The maid swung her arms wide to show how big the palace was, nearly hitting Mei's forehead in the process. "Why, there are at least...at least..." The maid scrunched up her eyebrows, deep in thought. "There are at least *twenty* people."

"Over eight hundred, actually."

"So you see, it's unlikely that one would know everybody!"

"But I do," insisted the princess. "I've memorized every single person in the palace."

The princess looked to be a little older than Mei, but not by much. She sat with perfect posture, her elegant sky blue robe draped over her legs and feet. Her hair was tied in a small bun and held in place with decorated chopsticks. She matched the rest of the room in its richness and finery—pearls glimmered on the small dressing table, which was lined with lacquered jewelry boxes and floral fans encrusted with precious stones. Mei had no doubt that just one of those lavish boxes or fans would translate to an entire week's food for the village back home. She began doing similar calculations with the other luxuries around her. *Beads of jade equal three pigs. Enameled hairbrush, three dozen chicken eggs.* It was a good way to keep her mind off the fact that she and Yun had been separated, and that she was now standing in a royal bedroom, mere feet from a real princess.

The maid reached for a pair of silver scissors on the dressing table. After she snipped the thread and sewed it onto the sleeve, she suddenly trilled, "Oh, no! No, no, no!"

"What's wrong, Miss Sha?" the princess asked calmly.

"I sewed it over the gold pattern here.... Oh, no, what should I do?"

"You should get the gold spool, Miss Sha."

"Yes, yes! I must get the gold spool!"

"Go. I'll wait."

The maid gave a deep bow, nearly tipping over in the process, then hurried from the room, leaving Mei alone with the princess. As soon as the maid was gone, the princess said helpfully, "There is a pincushion in the first drawer."

Mei blinked. She slowly removed all thirty-one pins from her mouth, squeezing them between her fingers, and carefully walked across the plush carpet to the drawer. A dainty purple cushion sat inside, poked with needles and pins. It looked like a silver porcupine.

Mei felt her cheeks flush. "Why did she make me hold the pins in my mouth, then?" she couldn't help blurting.

"Miss Sha's actually quite bright... when she pays attention," the princess said. "She's been distracted lately because she has to substitute for one of the other nursemaids, who caught the stomach flu. But even at her most scatterbrained, she isn't the worst. One time, one of my sisters put soap in my cup of tea by accident. She thought it was honey. I always tell people things will be much easier if they let me do things myself, but no one listens."

Mei finished pricking the cushion with the pins, then glanced at the open door. Miss Sha hadn't returned yet. Now was her chance to escape...except the maze-like hallways outside were lined with watchful officials and servants. And how was she supposed to find Yun? She hoped her brother wouldn't give them away—out of the two of them, there was no doubt he was the worse liar, obviously. Like the time he and Mei stole some candied nuts from the kitchen cupboard back home. They'd rehearsed beforehand what they'd say if the theft was discovered: "Smelly Tail knocked over the bowl and ate some." But when their parents asked, Yun had sung the truth like a bird on trial.

"You're new here, aren't you?" the princess asked.

Mei nodded hesitantly.

The princess smiled. "It's all right, I know it can be overwhelming at first. You'll get used to it, as all the other maids have."

The princess saw Mei eyeing her chopsticks and slid one out of her hair. "For self-defense," she said, revealing the chopstick's sharp metal end. "The men around here aren't the only ones carrying weapons."

To demonstrate how sharp the edge was, the princess lightly traced the curtain draped over her bed. The yellow fabric tore under the metal edge in one smooth easy stroke, as if it were made of flimsy paper. "Made it myself," the princess added.

Mei's mouth dropped. "Did you really?"

"What?" challenged the princess. "You don't think I'm capable of such a thing?"

"No, no, that's not what I meant," Mei hurried to say. "It's just—it's so beautiful." The chopstick had tiny blue-and-pink swirls and patterns, as if someone had painstakingly etched it with a single hair of a paintbrush.

A *whoosh* flew by Mei's ear, followed by the sound of a fine *crack*. Mei whipped her head. Embedded in the patterned wallpaper was the chopstick.

"Indeed," the princess said coolly. "The deadliest mushrooms in the mountains are often the prettiest ones, don't you know?"

Mei already knew that, of course. She admired the princess. Maybe they could have been friends, if they had grown up together in completely different circumstances. Her curiosity got the best of her. "Did you really mean it when you said you knew *everybody* here—Your Highness?" she added.

"No," the princess admitted. "I only memorized up to 882, and then I lost track. The palace is enormous. There are exactly 9,999 rooms. It's impossible for me to keep up with everyone, partly because I can no longer walk well." She shifted her legs from under her robe to show Mei.

Beneath the small, ornate slippers the princess wore, Mei saw that the princess's feet were bound in tight cloths so that they were as small as Mei's fists. Mei was hardly surprised; Mama once mentioned many daughters of the nobility had their feet altered this way. *People think girls ought to be dainty and fragile,* she had said disapprovingly.

Mei murmured an apology.

"I've gotten used to it," the princess said, tilting her head. "Since I cannot run about and get into mischief with my brothers and cousins, I spend most of my time designing personal weapons and reading." She motioned to her desk, which was full of half-scribbled notes and scrolls. "So, what's your name again?"

Mei hesitated, then decided on the nickname her mother often used for her. "My name's Mimi."

"I'm Princess Zali. It's a pleasure to meet you, Mimi. How long have you been at the palace?"

"Since today. To be honest...." Mei glanced at the door. "There's been a mix-up, you see. I'm not supposed to be here. I've been hired as one of the...the new bookkeepers for the palace."

"You take care of finances and money?" The princess looked skeptical. "That's what a bookkeeper does."

"No, I mean *books* keeper," Mei hurriedly said. "Of the place where they store all the books and stories, and records of past crimes and such."

"You mean the Imperial Library?"

"That's the one."

Princess Zali looked intrigued. "I didn't know they were hiring new...books keepers. You're very lucky. The library is splendid, but very few people are given access to it. It has records of almost everything that has happened in China and beyond, since the dawn of time."

"Do you go there often?" asked Mei.

"Yes, when I can. Even I have to be given permission by the emperor or empress. But I love it there."

"What's it like? How is it organized?"

Mei quickly realized she had gone too far with the questions. Princess Zali was staring at her with a calculating look.

The room was silent for a few seconds before the princess said quietly, "Surely the newly hired *books* keeper would know all this?"

"Right, sorry, it's only my first day and I haven't even been there yet." Mei laughed nervously and quickly changed the subject to the first thought that came to her. "Speaking of books and stories, have you heard the one of the City of Ashes?"

The princess raised an eyebrow. She opened her mouth to speak, but at that moment, Miss Sha returned humming with the gold spool. Miss Sha told the girls in great detail how much she loved the color gold ("It's the color of sunshine and happiness"), but how she liked blue just a teensy bit more ("And silver, too, but not as much as gold").

"All set," Miss Sha finally warbled. She brushed the princess's sleeves adoringly. Mei didn't see any difference from before. "You look *lovely*, Your Highness. It is time to go down to the banquet hall. Let me go fetch the carriers."

The maid disappeared a second time, leaving Mei alone with the princess once again. Princess Zali motioned for Mei to come closer.

"I *have* read about the City of Ashes, as a matter of fact," she said. "Legend says the place burned down after a poet's family was killed."

"Just her husband," Mei corrected.

"Oh?" said Princess Zali.

Encouraged by the princess's apparent interest, Mei explained that Lotus's husband had been framed by someone called the Noble General, and went into great detail about how the city had been cursed afterward. By the time she finished, Princess Zali's gaze was fixed so forcefully upon her that Mei suddenly felt rooted to the floor. "I heard about all this secondhand, of course," Mei quickly added.

"What's your name again?"

"Mei—Mimi," Mei said quickly, hoping her fierce blush didn't give her away. "Sorry, I-I should go. Don't want them to fire me on my first day. Off to the library I go!"

"And just how do you propose to do that?" the princess asked. "I'm curious because, as you'd surely know, the doors are sealed with an enchantment. As I said, most people are not permitted to enter without special permission. Even *books* keepers, who do most of their recordkeeping in an antechamber anyway."

"The library doors are *enchanted*?" Mei blurted before she thought better of it.

Princess Zali stared hard at Mei. "I think it is wise, *Mimi*, that you stay my personal maid for a while. Where I can keep an eye on you."

The princess's voice was suddenly dangerous. Mei stood still. Her eyes darted to the deadly chopstick wedged in the princess's hair.

"Y-Yes, Your Highness." Mei felt like kicking herself. Clearly she was a worse liar than she'd thought.

Two servants entered the room carrying a sedan chair. They lifted the princess from her bed and placed her on the seat.

"Until we meet again, then," the princess said, giving Mei a final measuring look. As they passed through the doorway, she snatched the chopstick in the wall and expertly placed it in her bun in one fluid movement.

CHAPTER FOURTEEN

十四

Two's Company, Three's a Crowd

Princess Zali had been right. The palace was enormous, with servants and workers bustling to and fro between the different buildings. It was a city in and of itself, with thousands of people—officials, servants, generals, and royal members of the family. The twins did not see each other that night, though unbeknownst to them, they often walked through the same place within moments of each other at the evening's dinner banquet.

Yun, whose arms were covered in burn marks and what looked like bird pecks, helped some of the chefs carry the dishes into the hall. As he aided Chef Fan with a particularly large pot of soup, Mei stood on the opposite end of the room with a stack of enameled bowls, ready to set the tables with the other maids.

The banquet, which was held in honor of a high official's birthday, was extravagant. The twins had never seen so much food in one place, not even during the Mid-Autumn Festival. Platters of dishes piled high kept coming from the kitchen, one after the other: soups, yellow and white noodles, steamed meats, pastries in all shapes and sizes. The rolls dripped with oil and gleamed like gold. At one point, a whole roast pig was carried out on an enormous plate.

There were at least eight courses and counting. The royal family members sat at long, elegant tables that could fit thirty each, surrounded by important officials and nobles and military leaders. Baba had once told Mei and Yun that the Imperial City comprised the most powerful people in all of China, and that sometimes conversations were extremely tricky, because you never wanted to offend the wrong person. The twins tried to imagine having a dinner conversation like that. It must be exhausting to be on guard all the time.

Yun was carrying out a plate of roast duck when he saw the familiar boy from before. Fu-Fu, Yun noticed, was sitting several tables away from the emperor's, which had bigger plates and larger portions than the rest. The boy kept looking glumly at the emperor's table, where several other kids sat. Yun recognized the look; he'd worn that same expression himself whenever the other village boys excluded him from their games.

Meanwhile, as Mei refilled soup bowls at table sixteen, she noticed Princess Zali often glanced around with a bored—and impatient—expression, nodding absentmindedly when her companions talked but clearly not listening to their words. The princess's mind was adventuring thousands of miles away. Mei wanted to go over and tell the princess she knew exactly how she felt, but decided it was best to lie low for now.

After the banquet, the twins were again herded in separate locations. That night, they were apart for the first time in their lives.

Yun crouched in his bunk bed in the servants' quarters. Above him, Chef Fan's loud snores shook the small room. Several other servants were on opposite bunks. Wisps of purple smoke rose above their heads.

Yun slowly tiptoed out of bed, then looked outside the window where the full moon shone in the sky.

"Where are you, Jade Rabbit?" he whispered.

There was no answer except Chef Fan's snores.

On the opposite side of the palace, Mei got up from her floor mat and sneaked past the other sleeping women in the maids' quarters, then looked outside the window at the same moon.

"What are we supposed to do now?" she asked the moon quietly.

Both siblings, though they didn't like to admit it, were afraid that night. When you've spent your entire life with someone, and then that person disappears, you feel as if you're all alone in the world. Everything seems stranger and darker than it was before.

✳

Making matters worse, the siblings could not find a way to communicate, much less locate each other in the gigantic city. During breaks before meal preparations began, Yun would wait at the place where they'd first arrived, hoping to spot Mei. But he kept drawing the attention of nosy servants (particularly the crane-like man, whose eyes were as sharp as the animal's). For her part, Mei left cryptic notes in random trees and behind statues, hoping her brother would find them, but the palace gardeners scrubbed the place so carefully that the notes were often found and discarded within minutes.

Over the next three days, the twins continued blending in as best as they could. Separated or not, they were resourceful children and knew the clock was ticking on their quest to clear Lotus's husband's name.

Yun didn't mind the blending part too much. He had always wanted to see life in the Imperial City, after listening to the stories Baba told. The palace chefs prepared hundreds of meals each day for all the members of the royal family. In the constant commotion, Yun's presence was easily overlooked, and he helped fetch the chefs' supplies and wheel in fresh vegetables from the city entrance. He learned tricks of the trade, like the fact that the broken, unlit hearth in the kitchen corner was actually a front for a tunnel that continued deep into the wall, leading to a hidden passageway to the marketplace outside. The pathway was used regularly by chefs who needed to fetch illegal and expensive delicacies after hours.

He also bonded in the kitchen with Chef Fan, who told him stories about his little girl.

"She used to get into all sorts of trouble," he chuckled as he sharpened his knife. "Sneaking around the premises with that bird of hers. She even managed to sneak into the royal family's quarters, believe it or not."

"How?"

"Maids and servants are the only people who can go anywhere without arousing suspicion. We're overlooked, like crickets on the sidewalk!"

Yun thought of something Grandpa had often told him. *A cricket can be smashed by a single footstep, yet its voice keeps up hundreds of folks at night. Even the smallest, most fragile among us have power, Yun.*

"So the servants are all treated badly here?" he asked, wondering how someone as boisterous as Chef Fan could be overlooked.

"Eh, just by a few really spoiled brats in the royal families," said Chef Fan with a shrug. "Not all of them are like that. There's one princess who always compliments me on my dishes, every single time. My daughter liked that girl a lot. Told me that princess had an arsenal of creative inventions up her sleeve. Could kill a grown man in her sleep."

"She sounds smart."

"Aye, they both were."

The crane man appeared. "I have a special order from one of the masters," he interrupted sternly. "He wants a hard-boiled egg that's runny on the inside, and a bowl of rice with every third grain salted and every fourth grain seasoned with sugar."

"Ridiculous!" cried Chef Fan.

"He has asked 'the skinny twelve-year-old chef' to prepare it." The crane-like man eyed Yun. "That means you. Get on it."

Yun groaned. "I bet it's that brat Fu-Fu." The day before, Fu-Fu had ordered Yun to serve him a bunch of grapes with the skins peeled. They had taken Yun an hour to prepare.

"Don't worry," said Chef Fan, whacking him on the back. "If you get started early, you might finish before sundown, you hear?"

Yun thought for a moment. "There's a faster way to do this than to count each individual rice grain," he said. "Watch this."

He rolled up his sleeves and divided up a bowl of rice into thirds. He salted one section.

"This is the same as dividing the bowl into twelve sections and salting four of them, or 4/12," Yun explained to a puzzled Chef Fan. He carefully divided the sections as such.

"Okay, so what about the sugared grains?" asked the chef.

"Every fourth grain sugared means one-fourth of the bowl, or 3/12," said Yun, and he sprinkled sugar over a quarter of the bowl as such.

Finally, he mixed all the rice in the bowl together—sugared, salted, and plain. "There," he said triumphantly. "Every third grain salted, every fourth grain sugared."

"Bravo," said the chef, impressed.

Yun smiled. He had beaten that brat at his own game.

*

Mei had imagined that royal life meant ample free time. But it turned out even the royal family had a strict regimen, especially the children—from daily lessons on writing and history to mandatory teatimes. Mei was kept busy in Princess Zali's quarters. She could tell the princess still distrusted her, yet, miraculously, she hadn't been arrested. She did her best to stay on Princess Zali's good side.

Fortunately, it wasn't hard. Princess Zali, as Mei found out, shared a lot of things in common with her.

"We have thousands and thousands of books here at the palace, not just in the library," the princess said as she concentrated on the scrolls on her writing desk. She was practicing her calligraphy while Mei dusted the room. "My favorite is *Journey to the West*. It's a story of the Monkey King's travels to obtain sacred texts, and the adventures he has along the way."

"I love the Monkey King!" said Mei, looking up from the figurine she was dusting. There were no books in her village, she explained, but she and her brother had heard countless adventures of the famous character from their parents and grandfather. Mei couldn't help but think once more that under different circumstances, she and the princess really could have been friends. She also had a gut feeling that was why the princess kept her around instead of having her arrested. As far as Mei knew, the princess hadn't even attempted to confirm Mei's story that she was hired as a bookkeeper.

"Yes, the story of the Monkey King is well-known folklore," said Princess Zali. "Other tales are not as memorable and fall through the cracks of history. It's interesting what stories are kept for centuries and what stories disappear over time."

"The Imperial Library has all of them, right?" piped up Mei nonchalantly. "I'd love to see it sometime, Your Highness. Oh, right, but there's the enchantment...."

Princess Zali gave Mei a knowing look. Before she could say anything, the door opened. Mei felt her heart sink.

Fu-Fu stood at the door.

He wielded his sharp stick and watched Mei with a smirk while the princess tried to concentrate on her calligraphy. For the last few days, the boy had popped up wherever Mei was, lurking in the courtyard or the gardens as she tended Princess Zali. He'd dangle the twins' bags in his hands tauntingly, as if to say, *Come and get it if you dare.*

There was a tense silence. Neither Fu-Fu nor Princess Zali greeted one another.

"You're not supposed to be here, Cousin Fu-Fu," Princess Zali finally said, looking up from her work. "How'd you get past the guards this time?"

"There are all sorts of secret passageways if you know where to look," said Fu-Fu with a yawn. "Besides, they can't stop me. *I* can walk anywhere I want, unlike some people." He started to dance about, swinging his sharp stick.

Princess Zali's face hardened. "Get out."

"How nice it must be to have people waiting on Your Royal Highness, to be *carried* everywhere. And to get brand-new clothes all the time. Isn't life *lovely* for little Princess Zali?"

"If you're worried because you're wearing one of your cousins' hand-me-downs, I assure you nobody cares," the princess replied calmly.

"You obviously care, since you noticed," shot back Fu-Fu, his face suddenly red. He glanced at Mei again. "Who's this, your new maid? You know she's not really a—"

"The princess said to get out," Mei said loudly before the boy could reveal anything else. She shoved Fu-Fu out the door.

"You're a fraud," Fu-Fu whispered, but he left with a sneer. The door swung shut behind him.

"Sorry about that, Your Highness," Mei said nervously. She wasn't sure why Fu-Fu hadn't reported her already. Whatever the reason was, it couldn't be good.

Neither of them spoke for a moment.

"I've been thinking about what you said the other day," the princess said. "The story of the City of Ashes, and the official who was responsible for the tragedy. I've read about him."

"Who, the Noble General?"

"Yes. I've thought a lot about what you told me. I've had my own suspicions about his role in the City of Ashes. Did you know he used to live there until its downfall, and then for the rest of his life back in the palace, he could only speak in riddles?"

Mei gave the princess a startled look. "He only spoke in *riddles* when he came back?" she repeated.

The princess paused, studying Mei's face. "Speaking of riddles, try to help me solve one right now. Very few people alive today know of the Noble General. I had to find information about him through archived palace memos. So, Mimi, I am curious how you knew of him. I'm curious how you know a lot of things, about Lotus and the City of Ashes."

Mei shrugged uncomfortably. Admitting that she got the information directly from the source seemed unwise. "Just rumors and such," she squeaked.

"Hmm. I do wonder about you, Mimi. You are not a book-keeper. You aren't an assassin, either, because you have yet to kill me." Princess Zali dipped her brush in the tiny ink bottle. "Of course, you can't, because I'd kill you before you could make a move," she added conversationally.

"Yes, Your Highness, I know," Mei said. "With your hair chopsticks."

"Not necessarily. I could just as easily dispatch you with *this*." The princess pointed to the dark liquid inside the ink bottle. "Ink is quite versatile. Depending on the ink's ingredients, it can be good for a variety of things. To make ink, you bake burnt soot, glue, and tree bark together until they're dried." She let the brush drip over the scroll. "I made this one myself. It has some added toxins from the venom of a snake. . . . One drop of this on your skin is enough to give you a second-degree burn. A big enough spatter would cause irrevocable poisoning. You'd be immobilized instantly."

Mei grinned in spite of herself. "That's impressive—I mean, dangerous, Your Highness." She quickly turned back to dusting the furniture.

The princess didn't say anything for a few moments. But a slow grin had spread over her face, too. "Thank you, Mimi. You are very kind."

✳

Working at the Imperial Palace tired out the twins more than fieldwork and schoolwork with Grandpa and their parents ever did. The third night, they went to bed earlier than everyone else.

Then something strange happened when they woke up.

It was morning again, but the rooms and hallways were empty.

Mei blinked and looked around for the other maids, but no one was around. The same thing happened on the opposite side of the palace where Yun was bunked. He called for Chef Fan and the others, but the hallways were quiet as tombs.

The twins raced through their respective quarters and out the doors. The sun was unusually bright—blinding, in fact. The courtyards were empty, too.

"Hello?" they shouted.

Across the distance, each sibling's call echoed as if they were right next to each other. They blinked. A moment later, they were standing across from each other, a mere few feet away.

The twins were too surprised and confused to say anything at first.

"What happened to you?" Mei finally said, eyeing the burn marks and what looked like bird pecks on Yun's arms.

"Don't ask," grumbled Yun. He rubbed his hands, which were raw from salting and smacking animal meats and bones over the last few days. But his grumpiness quickly vanished, replaced by relief. "*There* you are. I've been looking for you for days." He sniffed the air and wrinkled his nose. "Are you wearing perfume?"

"It was Princess Zali's. She let me try some. Where *is* everyone?"

"That's what I was wondering."

The desolate palace reminded the twins a little of the City of Ashes, except nothing was broken down here. In fact, everything seemed pristine, the colors brighter, the sky a shade of yellowish orange. Familiar wisps of colored smoke rose from the edges of their fields of vision, giving everything a distinctive blur, rather like Lotus's dream chamber.

"Yun," Mei gasped, making the connection aloud. "Are we . . . *dreaming?*"

"The exact same thing at the exact same time?" said Yun.

"It's not as if it hasn't happened to us before," Mei pointed out.

"I know, I know. It just feels different this time."

Mei understood what Yun was getting at. Until that moment, neither twin actually believed the other was truly *there* when they were dreaming. They'd always assumed that even if they were each dreaming the same thing, they were doing it independently.

Mei suddenly frowned. "Are you the *real* Yun?"

"What? Of course I am!"

Mei crossed her arms. "What's Baba's favorite food?"

"Come on, Mei, are you serious right now?"

"What's his favorite food?"

"Fried dumplings!"

"And Mama's is pickled cucumbers. All right, so you're real, more or less."

"That's . . . interesting, to say the least," said Yun. He knelt to inspect a fluttering flower. The blue petals opened and closed, as if winking. The flower's behavior seemed to make perfect sense. (That was the peculiar thing about dreams, how they feel perfectly normal even if you're being chased by a flying dragon.)

"Yes. And more importantly, we can communicate at last, after days apart! Hurry, before we wake up. Where have you been?"

Yun shared his stories of what had passed the last few days. As he did, the garden vanished. The twins found they were now standing in the imperial kitchen, next to the unlit hearths.

Then, when Mei told Yun her stories of Princess Zali, the kitchen was replaced by the princess's quarters, the colors in the bright room unusually muted. The yellow drapes over her bed were almost gray, the pieces of furniture mere shadows, as if someone had washed the colors out of them.

Their tales seemed almost like a dream itself, the fact they'd broken into the Imperial City and infiltrated its lower ranks. They laughed, sighed, and commiserated. When the subject of Fu-Fu came up, both twins rolled their eyes.

"He comes to bother the princess and me several times a day," Mei complained.

"He keeps asking me to do ridiculous tasks!" responded Yun. "I should've beaten him up when we had the chance."

"You've never beaten up anyone in your life."

"I surely could've, if not for the fact I choose to rise above such immature behavior."

"Sure," said Mei. "Well, don't worry, we'll get our stuff back somehow. The important thing is, what's our next move?"

"We have three days until Grandpa arrives," said Yun. "I haven't picked up any information about the City of Ashes by conversing or eavesdropping, so I think at this point I must resort to more aggressive tactics. I have some ideas on how to get a look at the records. They're rather complicated—"

"I have an idea too," Mei interrupted. "And it's rather simple. I'll ask Princess Zali to help us."

Yun's jaw dropped. "Are you out of your mind?"

"She's smart and capable and she's read about the City of Ashes. When I mentioned the Noble General, she seemed to know all about him." Mei shrugged, not quite knowing how to explain. "I just have a good feeling about her."

"You can't," argued Yun. "It's not safe to trust people here." He left out the part about how he'd accidentally revealed his own name to Chef Fan.

"We have to take a few risks if we're going to get anywhere, Yun. The important question is, Can we try to meet tomorrow when we're actually awake? Who knows how long this dream is going to last, or if it'll happen again."

"Good idea. The chefs were talking earlier about how there's a show for the palace children tomorrow evening after dinner."

"Where?" asked Mei, remembering Fu-Fu had mentioned something about the event, too.

"I don't know. But we could follow the crowd and meet backstage. I bet there will be lots of servants around. We wouldn't stick out."

"Agreed."

The twins were silent for a few moments as they stared at the clouds in the hazy sky. One of them looked oddly like the magic cloud the Jade Rabbit had conjured. In the back of their minds floated the pressing question, *What if I'm the only one dreaming this?* In the physical world, it was easy to tell what was real and what was in their imagination. In the dream world, that distinction was blurred.

"I wish Grandpa was here to answer our questions," Mei finally said. "I wish he could explain to us more about what's going on. With the fog. And the mooncakes. And this dream, and how we're able to talk to each other as if we were awake. As if this were...real."

"I guess before this, we never really had a need to talk to each other in our dreams," suggested Yun. "We were always together. We saw each other every day."

"Maybe," said Mei, frowning. "Most of all, I wish Grandpa didn't lie to us about our parents."

"He was trying to protect us," said Yun gently. "Plus, he didn't really know what had happened to our parents any more than we did, remember?"

"But grown-ups are supposed to know everything."

"They don't. They make mistakes just like us. They just hide it better."

"True..." agreed Mei.

When the twins blinked again, they were back in their beds. It was the middle of the night.

CHAPTER FIFTEEN

十五

A Royal Act

Dreams often fade away when you wake up. Many people have trouble remembering any of their dreams from the night before. Dreams aren't part of the physical world, after all.

When the twins woke up the next morning, however, their dream—and their plan to meet—stood out vividly in their minds. They completed their tasks anxiously throughout the day. Finally, after dinnertime, they followed the palace children and their caretakers to the evening's spectacle, which was held in an enormous theater.

Despite the crowd, the twins spotted each other backstage immediately and ran toward one another.

"Did we have the—" began Yun.

"—same dream?" finished Mei.

The twins were stunned. Something wondrous had happened, something that seemed impossible, yet to what end, they weren't quite sure. They thought of the Jade Rabbit's words about the dream world, and what it meant now that they had seemingly traveled through it consciously together the night before.

Before they could continue their conversation, several servants abruptly ushered the twins into a dressing room. Men in elaborate cloaks and painted faces roamed the space, tying up their hair and putting on makeup. A musician played the erhu, drawing out long, elegant, forlorn notes from the two-stringed instrument.

"You can't go onstage without costumes," said a performer carrying a tasseled broadsword. "Here, try these." He tossed the twins a pair of itchy costume robes—tacky green with peacock feathers for Mei, bright red the shade of Madam Hu's lipstick for Yun.

Bewildered, the twins hurried to explain they weren't actors. They started to head back out when the seemingly ever-present crane-like man stepped in front of them and blocked their path.

"As you will recall, earlier this week Master Fu-Fu requested the two of you perform in the show tonight," he said, crossing his arms. "In fact, he's pestered me about it daily."

"You mean we have to go *onstage*?" Yun said, his face pale.

"We don't know how to act," Mei tried to explain.

"That sounds like *your* problem." The crane man snapped his fingers at a nearby performer whose face had been painted into a green-and-red scowl. "Keep an eye on them so they don't sneak out. I have better things to do tonight than to babysit whiny servants."

After he left, the green-and-red man tried to cheer the twins up. "It's a variety show for the royal children," he said. "Anything goes! Tell a story or sing a song."

Mei and Yun knew plenty of stories from Grandpa, and some from their parents. Somehow, Mei and Yun didn't think this particular crowd would appreciate a simple story without singing or dancing. And the only songs the twins knew were ones they'd learned as toddlers, tunes that were full of clapping hands and nonsensical rhymes about farm animals. The twins had not met any professional actors in their life at the village. They'd heard of traveling acting troupes, but had never seen one in person.

"Acting's not that hard, either," continued the performer. "I've been doing it for years. There is something magical about acting. An individual steps into character and becomes absolutely anything they want, be it a dragon rider, a demon, a decrepit tree. The timid are suddenly bold, the fearless suddenly meek. Combine acting with storytelling and music, and you get hours of entertainment that enchants a crowd."

"A crowd," muttered Yun, looking queasy.

"Come on, it might not be that bad," urged Mei. She peeked behind the velvet curtain at the audience. There were at least a hundred people, perhaps thirty of them children. She spotted Fu-Fu waiting impatiently in the front row, wielding his ever-present bamboo stick.

"No way." Yun shook his head vigorously. "We need to remain inconspicuous, keep a low profile. Going onstage is the opposite of that!"

"Unfortunately, we might get arrested if we *don't* go onstage," Mei responded grimly. A small, sleepy toddler in the second row had caught her attention. There appeared to be a faint, soft blue mist forming above the toddler's head. The mist drifted over the nearby audience members before vanishing, the way smoke from a match disperses into thin air. Something about the familiar color reassured Mei.

She walked over to a trunk holding miscellaneous props. It held all sorts of interesting and odd objects: hoops, matches, wooden puzzle boxes, fake swords, and gaudy necklaces only someone like Madam Hu would wear. She dug through the trunk, then took out two wooden toy swords. "How about we duel for the audience?" she suggested. The swords weren't real, but at least they were an upgrade from the branches they normally used.

"No thanks," Yun said flatly.

Mei rummaged the trunk and extracted a small brown pouch. "I wonder what this is?"

She pulled back the drawstring on the pouch. An explosion of gold glitter filled the air.

"On second thought," she said, coughing, "maybe we can just read a nice poem."

"You won't find any at the palace," said the green-and-red-faced performer. "Written poems are hard to come by around here."

"Why's that?" Yun asked.

The elderly actor took a deep breath. "Well, as the story goes, there once was a high official from decades ago who hated poets with a passion. Said poems were 'dangerous.' He tried to burn all the poetry scrolls and books he could find, and even went so far as to suggest to the previous emperor that the palace's entire poetry collection be destroyed."

"That's ridiculous," said Yun. "Our fath—someone we know was a scholar here, and he never mentioned that the palace's poetry had been destroyed."

"That's because the previous emperor did the exact opposite," said the actor with a wink. "He had the poetry safeguarded in the Imperial Library, just in case the official got any ideas. I guess his son hasn't remembered to bring it back out again since he ascended the throne. I hope he will one day, though."

"That high official sounds awful," said Mei.

"Oh, yes, he was an absurd fellow. You know how the famous saying goes: *Better to be a salamander than a babbling commander.*"

"I'd never heard that until a few days ago," said Yun, who knew many famous quotes.

"Oh, maybe it's just a saying around here in the palace. You young ones wouldn't have any reason to know this, but it refers to that particular official. He only spoke in riddles until the end of his life."

At those words, Mei's suspicions were confirmed. She pulled her brother aside and quietly relayed what Princess Zali had told her about the Noble General.

Yun looked stunned. "Impossible."

"The official's long dead now," said the actor with a dismissive wave of his hand. "Not a lot of people remember him anymore. I only knew of him briefly when I was younger."

Mei and Yun glanced at each other. This could be a chance for information—maybe a big one.

"What else do you remember, exactly?" Yun asked, trying to keep calm.

"About the babbling commander? Well...he was not well-liked in his time. He was pushy and rude, and, as I understand it, he liked to blackmail people. He hadn't always spoken in riddles—that was the odd thing. The riddles came out of nowhere.... After that, he spent his later years in hiding."

"Hiding?" Mei repeated.

"Yes, hiding. Barricaded himself in his office over in the palace's military wing. People say he went off the deep end."

"From what I hear, he at least had excellent penmanship," said a voice behind the twins. They turned to see the performer with the broadsword standing nearby. He smiled and said, "My grandfather was a palace messenger. He told me all about his job when I was growing up, and I remember him talking about that official. The official went by some pompous name—the General Noble or something like that. Apparently, he'd write out orders on pieces of paper."

"Huh," said the twins.

"Makes sense, doesn't it, if that's the only way you can communicate? No one could understand him otherwise, when the riddling got bad. Almost makes you feel sorry for the man."

"Tough luck," agreed the first performer. "Anyhow, I wish we could see all those poems that got locked away. I'll bet we could create a lot of good performances around them."

"Why don't you ask for them to be brought out?" asked Yun. "It's been years and years."

"Because I'm just a lowly performer," said the actor, confused.

"We can't simply ask the emperor to do something,"

explained the broadsword performer. "People like us have very little influence in the palace."

"Everyone's voice is valuable," argued Yun. "They are all necessary for a functional society—"

"First-act jugglers in position!" a servant suddenly called. "The show begins in three...two...one!"

Yun looked at Mei in alarm. "What are we going to do again, exactly?"

Mei also seemed nervous. "We'll just have to wing it, I guess."

"Improvisation, I love it!" the actor said to the twins with a wink. "Good luck. No offense, you're going to need it. Children are some of the sharpest critics in the world. You can fool an adult, but you can't fool a kid!"

※

Out in the palace theater, the lanterns dimmed, and the audience fell silent. Mostly silent. The younger children, especially those under the age of four, had yet to master the art of sitting still and not giggling every five seconds.

A few times a year, the imperial court held an evening show for all the children at the palace. One of the emperor's officials had explained it was held so that the young minds "could develop a deep, curated appreciation for the fine art of theater," but some of the older children suspected the show was likely just to keep them entertained while the servants inspected their quarters for stolen treasures and contraband. (Indeed, the year before, one of the kids found that his hidden stash of firecrackers went missing, and the next morning the palace guards had held an impromptu fireworks display.)

Fu-Fu sat on his velvet seat cushion in the front row with a bored expression. The nine-year-old didn't enjoy sitting still for too long. His arms and legs were always jittery, itching to climb a pillar or to run down a long corridor looking for trouble. He loved finding trouble: stealing a mooncake, smearing dirt on the carpets, sneaking somewhere he shouldn't. Trouble was fun. Everything else was so *boring*.

"Be quiet, the show's starting!" one of the supervising aunts hissed. Two of Fu-Fu's cousins—Cousin Big-Nose and Cousin Jabber, he called them—stopped their whispering in the second row.

None of the cousins spoke to Fu-Fu, and that was just as well, because Fu-Fu didn't like hanging out with any of his cousins. That was why he was especially delighted when he ran into the strange siblings earlier that week. He knew they weren't supposed to be there. Probably beggars or orphans, or perhaps assassins and spies—although the contents of their bags proved the former was more likely. They contained nothing significant except for an old porcelain jar, and even that was boring. The Imperial City had thousands that were much nicer.

The bags now lay at his feet, and he kicked them absentmindedly as he waited. The guards would surely arrest the twins as soon as he tipped one off about the trespassers. So far, however, Fu-Fu had not told anyone. Not yet. He'd decided to save that moment for the end of the performance, when he'd have his own big finale—a great reveal—and come out the hero. Then he'd show whiny Cousin Jabber who was boss. He'd show them all that he didn't have to be related to the emperor to achieve greatness. That he didn't need to have the best food or toys or maids and servants. Fu-Fu, the mere great-grandson of a high official, was just as good as the best of them.

The stage lit up. The first performance was a juggling act. The audience clapped politely.

The second performance was a sword swallower. The act made all the younger children gasp, and made the older kids tremble uneasily. They all watched in silence as the performer slowly sank the tip of the broadsword down his throat, inch by inch, until only the colored tassels around the pommel were left.

"Do *not* try this at home!" the aunt reminded the audience sternly. "You will slit your throat as though it were a slice of raw tofu."

Now, every kid shuddered.

The third and fourth acts were parts of an old Chinese opera. It was mildly interesting, but Fu-Fu was getting restless. Where were the twins he had asked for? He started to wonder whether the pesky servants had obeyed his orders.

Just then, a hush fell over the audience. Fu-Fu sat up straight.

The boy from the strange sibling pair was slowly walking onstage, his gait stiff and jerking. He looked woodenly at the audience. His pale lips mumbled something no one could hear.

Confused murmurs emerged in the audience.

"It's a human puppet!" a six-year-old from the front squealed.

"No, dummy, he's obviously real," Cousin Sharp-Tongue replied. "He's just pretending to be a statue."

"Statues don't move, stupid!" Cousin Big-Nose called out.

"Did you call me stupid?"

"No, *he's* stupid."

While the aunts tried to get the kids to settle down, the boy's sister ran onstage. "That, everyone, was called the Walking Corpse!" she laughed (a bit forcefully, Fu-Fu thought). "Give it up for this brilliant actor!"

After the unenthusiastic clapping died down, the girl smiled and announced she was going to duel an invisible swordsman. She held up a toy sword and began whipping it back and forth, ducking and jumping here and there. Her movements were smooth and fast, and remarkably skilled, but watching someone duel an invisible opponent is about as much fun as watching someone jog in place. A few minutes later, the audience grew restless again. The girl's brother stood silently beside her, as though he forgot how to move or talk. Perhaps he was mimicking a statue after all.

"This stinks!" booed Fu-Fu.

The aunts scolded him, but not before a flurry of snickers spread through the audience. Mei glared at Fu-Fu. Without a pause, she threw the sword down and marched forward on the stage.

"For my next act, I need a volunteer from the audience," she said.

The room oohed. They'd never seen an interactive show before. Excitement rippled through the audience. The younger children shot their arms into the air, pleading, "Pick me! Pick me!"

Mei swept her gaze over the audience. "I'll pick"—she paused for dramatic effect—"*that* boy." She pointed straight at Fu-Fu. "You."

Fu-Fu felt his face burn, but he stuck out his chin and pretended to act nonchalant. "Me?" he sneered.

"Yes. I need you to hand me those bags you have."

The boy flinched. "I don't know what you're talking about."

"Those, the ones right beside your bamboo stick."

He immediately regretted bringing those twits' bags with him to the theater. "I don't have to give you anything," he replied.

But the aunts and cousins were all eagerly waiting for him to obey the performer's orders.

"Maybe she'll turn them into puppets!" cheered the same six-year-old.

Another cousin suggested the performers were going to guess what was inside the bags, which prompted several of the kids to debate whether Cousin Fu-Fu was in on the act.

"That's not fair," Cousin Jabber called out, slamming his fist. "I'm third in line to the throne. How come *I'm* not picked?"

Cousin Jabber's outrage was what prompted Fu-Fu to agree in the end. He tossed the duffel bags onstage.

"Thank you," said Mei, snatching the bags. She turned to her brother and said in a low whisper, "Let's get out of here."

"Hey, wait a minute!" yelled Fu-Fu, who had heard her. "They're getting away with my stuff!"

In her haste, Mei accidentally dropped one of the duffel bags. The porcelain jar rolled out, and the cap fell off with a clatter.

Some of the cousins whispered to one another with puzzled glances. *Did Cousin Fu-Fu own that thing? Impossible, he only gets hand-me-downs. . . . Perhaps he stole it from one of the princes or princesses. . . . We should check our rooms when we get back.*

"I didn't steal it from any of you," Fu-Fu retorted hotly above the murmurs.

"Shh!" hissed one of the aunts, and the crowd fell silent again. They watched the girl onstage, who was wrestling with the jar.

She popped the lid back on. "B-Behold!" She nervously laughed. "I call this the magic storm cloud! Don't worry, it will dissipate."

Except there was nothing onstage that the audience could see. The girl caught the crowd's confused looks and pointed to the air. "It's right here. Look! Don't you see the green-and-black cloud?"

"And lightning," croaked her sibling, who still stood as rigid as a puppet.

A few uncertain giggles hiccupped in the crowd. The royal audience was not used to performances of such low quality. To make matters worse, Cousin Baby-Tooth had fallen asleep again in the second row and let out an enormous, well-timed snore. Within seconds, the whole room erupted in laughter.

One of the aunts suggested the next performer come onstage in the interest of moving things along. The girl put the jar away, her cheeks fiery red. She nudged her companion, who woodenly began following her offstage.

"I want my bags back!" Fu-Fu called loudly.

"No, they're not his—" the girl began to say, but one of the previous performers had already wrestled the bags from her hands. He presented them to Fu-Fu with a slight bow.

"That's more like it." Fu-Fu was glad for the opportunity to display his power, especially in front of the newcomers. He puffed out his chest and said to the siblings, "You two can sit next to me and watch the rest of the show from the first row. I'm such a nice guy." He grinned at the girl. "Aren't I?"

The girl glared at him. "We'll find our own seats, thanks." With one last furious scowl, she tugged her sibling along, and they disappeared offstage, nearly toppling the musician and his erhu waiting in the wings.

CHAPTER SIXTEEN

十六

The Phoenix Seal

While the musician performed, Mei tiptoed through the audience to find Princess Zali. Yun was still recovering backstage from the disastrous performance, and Mei had taken this opportunity to slip away on her own. Fueled by frustration, Mei had made a decision. The prince would be arriving with Grandpa in two days. Whatever complicated tactics her twin had in mind to get at the records in the Imperial Library by then, Mei was doubtful he'd be able to move fast enough. Princess Zali was their only hope.

She spotted the princess sitting all the way in the back of the theater by herself; her attendants stood a good distance away. *Perfect.* Mei quietly approached her.

"Sorry to interrupt, Your Highness," she whispered. "I would like to speak with you in private, if I may."

The princess nodded. "That was an...interesting...act you did. Invisible clouds, huh?"

"Something like that, sure," Mei grumbled. It was like back at the village again, when she and Yun were the only kids who could see the fog. She wanted to kick herself for making the same mistake here in the Imperial City.

"Who was that boy with you? Where is he?"

"He's nobody." Mei couldn't believe she had such a useless sibling. She had almost succeeded in getting their belongings back from Fu-Fu, while Yun had frozen like a block of ice. Moreover, their performance was the opposite of forgettable; they probably stood out like sore thumbs. Now they'd be more recognizable around the palace because of it. And their bags—and Grandpa's jar—were gone. Again.

"Maid, bookkeeper, and actress. You're a woman of many talents, Mimi." There was a lull in the music. Princess Zali waited for the strings to play again, then leaned in and said, "So what did you wish to discuss with me?"

"I wanted to talk to you about..." Mei wished more than anything to tell the princess the truth. She knew Yun didn't want her to, but Yun wasn't here, and they were running out of time. Mei took a deep breath. "Truth is, I'm not a maid or a bookkeeper."

The princess motioned for Mei to move in closer. "I thought not. Who are you, then?" Her expression was kind and curious.

Perhaps against her better judgment, Mei admitted quietly, "I'm an outsider. I snuck into the palace with my brother, who was onstage with me. We're from a village down south."

The princess placed her hand on Mei's shoulder. At first,

Mei thought it was simply a kind gesture, until she felt something faint and sharp pressed against her neck. She saw the end of the gleaming chopstick between Princess Zali's fingers.

"Reveal your true identity," the princess breathed calmly. "Or I'll be commanding the guards to bury your body."

Alarmed, Mei rushed to explain. "M-My name's Mei Wu. My brother and I are from a village in the mountains. Our village—" She paused, then figured she was locked into the truth at this point. She waited until the erhu player was playing a particularly loud melody, then whispered, "Our village has been cursed—by the same curse that befell the City of Ashes. We went there and met the spirit who caused the destruction there. The poet called Lotus. She told us she'd lift the curse if we prove her husband was framed and wrongly executed."

She winced. What she'd just said sounded like pure gibberish out loud. She might as well have admitted they'd made a deal with a talking animal and had a jar of dreams. If the princess wasn't going to kill her for being an intruder, certainly she'd lock her up for being a dangerous lunatic now.

For several long moments, there was only the sound of the erhu strings.

"You say you're from a cursed village in the mountains?" repeated Princess Zali.

"Yes," Mei said, trembling. "The curse started in the City of Ashes. It spilled over to our village somehow. During the Mid-Autumn Festival, the emperor's son visited and wrongly arrested our grandpa for serving him bad mooncakes. That's another thing. They're on their way back here. I don't know what your brother has planned for Grandpa, but he's innocent. We *have* to set him free when they arrive in two days."

Princess Zali lowered her hand, revealing the glint of the weapon, then slowly drew herself up. One of the nearby maids approached to ask if she was alright.

"I have to use the chamber pot," she calmly answered. Two servants started to rush over, but the princess gave them a terse shake of the head. "I have a helper already," she said, motioning toward Mei. "She will assist me."

Mei nervously helped the princess walk out the theater doors. Out in the empty corridor, Princess Zali took tiny steps until she leaned against the balcony overlooking the courtyard. Out on the lawn, a group of men were practicing martial arts in the moonlight—their kicks and punches identical and precise, no arm or leg raised too low or too high. The princess watched them longingly for a few moments. Then she folded her arms and gave Mei a stern look.

"I suppose this—this *quest* of yours is why you've been so interested in the Imperial Library? You'll be wanting to look at the historical records, won't you?"

"That's right," squeaked Mei.

"Why did you lie to me?"

"I'm sorry. I couldn't tell you the truth, Your Highness."

"You don't have to call me that. We're practically the same age." The princess took a deep breath. "Back up a bit. How did you arrive? Did you come straight from the City of Ashes?"

Mei told her about the journey from the village to the City of Ashes, and the magic cloud that took her and Yun to the Imperial City. Princess Zali stared at her, as if deciphering whether she was telling the truth.

"If you are lying to me, you wouldn't tell such an outrageous story," she said after a moment. "Therefore...this all must be true."

"It is. I swear."

"Where are your parents?"

Mei couldn't answer. Princess Zali seemed to understand.

"I ought to report you, if not outright kill you," the princess said, her voice hard. "But I won't."

"You won't report me? Or kill me?"

"Both."

Mei was too relieved and astonished to reply.

"It's mighty impressive what you've done," continued Princess Zali quietly. "I've never done what you have. I've never been part of...of an adventure like that."

Mei thought of how she did not choose this particular adventure, to have her village cursed, her grandpa arrested, and her parents frozen in time. "I didn't have a choice," she admitted.

The princess replied, "You could've stayed home and hidden, but you didn't. You chose to venture into the unknown. I'm the one who doesn't get a choice in anything."

"But..." Mei knew she shouldn't interrupt, but she couldn't help herself. "But everyone here listens to you. You give orders, and they obey."

"Sure, I ask for things, and people bring them to me. But that's not the same as having freedom."

Mei looked at her questioningly, and Princess Zali looked out at the practicing soldiers again. The men had taken a break, and they were laughing together. Long, musical notes floated from inside the palace theater. The princess's eyes lowered.

"Being a princess means every part of your life's controlled. More so, when you can't walk well. You're always surrounded by people waiting on you all the time, bringing you food, making sure you're dressed comfortably. You can't even get a drink of water without five people fumbling over you. Almost like you're an infant."

Mei remembered how Miss Sha had fawned over Princess Zali with the threads, stitches that the princess could've done herself easily. She also remembered Princess Zali and Fu-Fu's exchange back in her bedroom, and she wondered if the princess dealt with that kind of teasing constantly.

"Don't get me started about my parents' and other people's expectations. *No, Princess Zali, you cannot join your brothers in physical combat. No, Your Highness, women must not run or shout from the rooftops.*"

This last reproach sounded familiar to Mei, and she felt a pang of sympathy for the princess.

"For once, I want to be myself. Not the perfect princess people expect me to be." Princess Zali raised her eyes to meet Mei's. "Maybe tonight, I can take my first step, metaphorically speaking."

She made sure no one was in the hallway, then took out a folded paper from under the silk pink sash around her waist. She smoothed out the paper's edges and showed it to Mei. On it was an intricate sketch of a map of the Imperial City with all its buildings and yards.

"I drew this myself," Princess Zali said. "I keep it with me at all times to study the layout of the city and memorize it—and imagine myself going wherever I please. I think it will help you with your quest." She pointed to a building she'd circled. "This is the Imperial Library, inside the Pavilion of Literary Wisdom." Dashed lines surrounded the square room. The princess explained the lines represented the protective enchantment.

"What is the enchantment?" asked Mei.

"The enchantment prevents anyone but those given the emperor's permission from going inside the library. It alerts my father to any trespasser's presence. Too many officials try to sneak in to rewrite history and modify records. But this is where you want to go. It has thousands of records pertaining to the histories of every city in China. All recorded arrests are there."

Mei blinked at the map, then at Princess Zali. "You're helping me, then?" she whispered.

"It's not every day you hear about a quest to appease the spirit of a vengeful poet in a haunted city. I want to be part of your adventure, too." The princess gave a small smile. "So yes, I'm helping you. But only to a point, I'm afraid. Ideally, I would access the records for you, but to get permission to enter the library, I'd need to request an audience with my father. Then he'd get one of his messengers to write the permission slip and assign select carriers to accompany me. It'd take at least a week, if not longer. I suspect you need access *much* sooner."

She placed the paper in Mei's hand. An understanding passed between them.

"I've highlighted the passageways that are rarely used," added Princess Zali.

Mei was glad she'd followed her instincts about the princess. "So how do my brother and I get into the library, if it's locked with an enchantment?"

"Here's the thing. The enchantment doesn't affect the emperor himself. Or the empress."

"You're going to ask *them* to help us?"

"Don't be ridiculous. What would they say if I told them two shady vagabonds broke into the palace in order to save a cursed village?"

"Right."

"What you need is Mother's seal," said Princess Zali.

"The empress's . . . seal," repeated Mei slowly, not wanting to admit she was completely lost.

"She keeps a copy in her quarters," said the princess with a nod. "If you carry it on you, the enchantment shouldn't affect you. That is my best guess."

"And I'm supposed to *ask* her for it?"

Princess Zali scrunched her eyebrows. "Mei, my mother doesn't even give *me* the seal when I ask for it."

The thought of sneaking into the Empress of China's quarters and stealing from her alarmed Mei. "I can't do that!" she cried.

"Well, I see no other way. I'd do it myself, except I'm nowhere as fast as you. Think about it this way: you've already broken fifty rules by infiltrating the Imperial City and impersonating a maid. Or 'books keeper,' as you claimed. Besides, lifting a curse from a village—and a whole city— seems like it's worth taking the risk, don't you think?"

"Yes, I suppose," Mei said uncertainly. Then, louder, "Yes, it is."

Princess Zali pointed to the map again. "Mother's quarters are the third door down the first hallway from my room. The seal is hidden in the bottom drawer of the dresser on the left, next to a jade statue of a phoenix. She is currently having evening tea with some officials, so you have"—the princess squeezed her eyes shut in thought—"thirty-nine minutes to complete the task."

Mei rushed to memorize the instructions. "Sorry, what does the seal look like?"

"It's a seal of a phoenix. You'll recognize it right away. It's the most valuable item in the drawer."

Mei hesitated. "I should check with my brother first, to see if he's onboard with the plan—"

"Thirty-eight minutes."

"All right, all right! We'll try our best."

"Good. Remember that I am placing enormous trust in you. If people find out I'm assisting two thieves to steal Mother's seal, I might as well jump in a vat of boiling oil."

"I won't let you down," promised Mei.

"Take the hallway to the right," said Princess Zali. "The only person on duty is a servant who likes to get tipsy during these performances. If you run into anyone who questions your presence, tell them to bring you to me."

"Thank you, Your High—I mean, Zali."

The princess squeezed Mei's hand, then let go. "Help me walk back into the theater. Act normally. Then get your task done and save your village."

✳

Mei, flushed with nerves and excitement, hurried backstage. Yun, for his part, had recovered enough from his lapse onstage that when his sister quietly explained their next steps, he kept his bitter thoughts to himself, and grudgingly slipped away with her into the corridors without arguing. Not a lot of people were on guard duty the night of the children's play; it was a holiday for the entire palace. Indeed, the only obstacle was a servant snoring outside the theater doors. The twins scurried down the hallway and out into the courtyard.

"This way," said Mei, pointing to the map Princess Zali had drawn.

The sound of chirping crickets filled the courtyards. Above, the moon glinted off the sloped rooftops and guided their path in the dark. Mei and Yun wondered if the Jade Rabbit was secretly watching them overhead. It had been seven days since the Mid-Autumn Festival, and the moon no longer was full, but a crescent, like a slice of orange.

Under the cloak of night, they snaked past the many different buildings around them and made their way to the northern side of the palace complex. They stuck to the lesser-trekked passageways that the princess had highlighted. Mei took the lead on surveying corners, making sure no one was around. Yun trailed behind her reluctantly, mumbling that this was a bad idea.

They managed to head back through the empty royal quarters. Since all the royal children were at the performance, the hallways were empty. Mei retraced her steps to the princess's room, then followed the instructions given to her.

"First hallway, third door," she said.

Yun grumbled under his breath. "I still don't think we should trust the princess," he insisted. "Why did you tell her the truth?"

"Because she's like us, in many ways."

"Um, Mei, you're talking about a *princess* in the *imperial court* of China. That's like comparing a butterfly to a gnat."

"Fine then, don't trust her. But at least trust me." Mei's voice was tinged with annoyance. "Besides, it was a good thing I did," she added. "I was able to find out information about the library and its enchantment."

"*I* could have told you that!" said Yun, exasperated. "Everyone who's read the history of the imperial courts knows the Imperial Library is locked with an enchantment, and only the emperor and empress can enter with special seals. Baba even told us so, remember?"

Mei didn't answer.

Yun started to say something more, then decided it wasn't worth it. His sister's memory had never been as good as his own. Mei often went by gut instinct; Yun went by memorization and strategy. It was one of the things that used to frustrate him whenever they played games. One time, in an infamous game of backgammon with the other village kids, Mei lost her and Yun's entire pot because she refused to listen to Yun's advice. "It was just bad luck," she'd said dismissively, to which Yun had argued that backgammon was a game of skill, and they'd have won if she had been paying attention like he was.

They started to turn into the corridor, then blanched. Two guards were heading toward them from the other end. The guards were deep in an argument and did not seem to notice the twins. In that valuable split second, Mei and Yun jumped back around the corner and knelt in the shadow. They held their breath, the noise of their pounding hearts drumming in their ears.

The voices of the guards grew louder as they approached.

". . . your own fault for betting such a priceless heirloom," one of the guards was saying.

"How was I supposed to know he'd cheat?" the other guard argued.

"Doesn't matter. You should never bet anything you can't live without, especially in a card game. Anyway, you don't know if he cheated."

"I'll bet he did. He *always* wins, that sneaky rat…or should I say crane?"

The second guard laughed. "Mm-hmm, he *does* look like a bird."

Mei and Yun remained still. It was too late to run for the exit. They could only hope against hope that the guards wouldn't turn toward their direction as they passed.

The guards rounded the corner, armed with bows and arrows on their backs and heavy swords at their sides. They disappeared down the other end, still squabbling. Mei and Yun waited until their voices completely faded down the hallway.

"That was too close," Yun muttered, wiping his forehead.

"Let's hurry." Mei led the way and stopped in front of the third oak door down the hall. "This one."

They stood still for a few moments, then Yun cautiously knocked on the door. Nobody answered. Quietly, as Yun muttered under his breath about how they *really* shouldn't do this, Mei pushed on the door.

It was locked.

"Uh-oh," mumbled Mei. "I think Princess Zali forgot about this part."

Yun swallowed. "This is what always happens," he said through clenched teeth. "You never think ahead. It didn't occur to you to ask the princess about the door to the empress's quarters?"

"Give me a break, Sir He-Who-Freezes-Like-a-Dummy-Onstage."

Yun's expression hardened as he moved Mei aside to examine the doorknob. He knelt down until his eye was in line with the keyhole. It was the size of his thumb. The grooves inside didn't seem overly complicated.

"Maybe the princess didn't forget," Yun said after a moment. "She probably assumed we could get past this locked door, if we've been sneaking around the Imperial City. Although we haven't *actually* been picking any locks . . . until now." His gaze landed on Mei's butterfly pin. "Let me borrow that."

Mei reluctantly handed over their mother's hairpin.

Yun slid the sharp end of the hairpin into the keyhole. Picking a lock requires mostly concentration, but having good close-up vision proves significant advantage. Yun was able to see the grooves that lined the inside of the lock. His keen ears were also able to hear whether the faint *click* of the mechanism worked. He moved the pin slowly, carefully.

At last, the door slid open.

They stepped into the empress's chamber. It was as beautiful as Princess Zali's had been, but bigger and even more lavish. There was not a spot in the room that was bare; every spare inch was adorned with red silk wallpaper or plush carpet, or else was brimming with artifacts. There was a long desk with glittering beauty supplies: tiny pillows of face powder, scarlet red lip paint, gilded combs. Mei instinctively thought of Mama, and whether any of these held the same magic as her butterfly pin.

Next to a sleek statue of a phoenix was the dresser that

the princess had told Mei about. While Yun groaned over and over, "I can't believe we broke into the Empress of China's quarters," Mei hurried to the dresser and tugged on the bottom drawer. It wouldn't budge. She tried the upper drawers, which opened easily.

"The bottom one's jammed!" she grunted.

Yun studied the polished wooden drawers carefully. They didn't seem to have any keyholes. "Let me borrow the hairpin again."

Sometimes the drawer in their father's desk also became jammed whenever a scroll got caught in the side. Yun stuck the pin into the narrow side space of the empress's drawer. After a few swishes, Yun plucked out a crumpled paper-thin scarf that had wedged itself behind the drawer. It then opened with ease, revealing exquisite green jade pearls, pendants, and black onyx beads.

"We're looking for a seal of a phoenix," said Mei, ignoring her brother's slightly smug smile. "It's the most valuable item in the dresser."

She reached for a flat pendant that had the imprint of a dragon, tossed it aside, grabbed a tiny seahorse molded from smooth stone, tossed *that* aside, then held up a fistful of loose gold coins. Funnily enough, every single item seemed like it could be the most valuable item in there.

"We need to get out of here soon," Yun reminded her.

"I'm hurrying!" snapped Mei.

She dug deeper through the drawer of treasures. There were multiple seals inside: a circular seal of a peacock, a tiny seal of a serpent with jade beads for the eyes, even a seal depicting a rabbit raising its head toward the moon (it did not resemble the real Jade Rabbit particularly well; its hind paws were much too small). Her fingers curled around a heavy silver square. As soon as she felt it, she knew it was the right one.

"Look." She revealed the item gleaming in her palm. Engraved on the square was an image of a phoenix, its wings spread over its head.

It was the empress's seal.

CHAPTER SEVENTEEN

十七

The Magical Library

The twins crossed a short marble bridge on the southern side of the palace complex and reached the pavilion. The single-story building looked almost shabby in comparison to its neighbors; there were no gilded roofs, no gleaming columns. But looks were often deceiving.

They entered the unguarded hall (for who needs guards when there's a protective magical enchantment in place?), went past the giant bronze statues, then down a long corridor. At the end of the corridor was a pair of heavy-looking doors. The left had a giant blue-green emblem of a coiled dragon, the other, a phoenix. The phoenix matched the one on the empress's seal.

Mei's skin prickled. She hesitated, not completely sure if they should go through with the task after all. Breaking through a locked door was one thing. Breaking past enchanted doors was something else entirely. Nothing was off the table when magic was involved.

Yun, sensing her hesitation, said, "We've gotten this far. No point in turning back now, unfortunately."

"Here goes nothing, then," Mei muttered.

She held the empress's seal up to the towering doors. She felt a tingle shoot up her arm. Hoping that was a good sign, she squeezed the seal and pushed on the wooden phoenix above her. The door to the Imperial Library slid forward with a loud groan.

The windowless room was dim, the only light coming from the soft glow of lanterns in the corners. Dark oak shelves of worn books and scrolls lined the paneled walls— thousands upon thousands of scrolls. The place seemed to have no ceiling, as some of the bookshelves were several stories high, the topmost rows fading into the dark and looking no bigger than the twins' thumbs.

Their mouths agape, they walked deeper into the room. With each step, more bookshelves, display cases, and tables appeared to materialize out of thin air. The room seemed never-ending.

"Where do we start?" asked Mei.

"Anywhere, I guess." Yun carefully unfurled a scroll from a nearby shelf and studied the Chinese characters. It was a list of dates and what the past emperors ate for dinner each night. He put the scroll back, then unrolled another one. That one was a list of palace officials and their birthdays.

They browsed different sections of the library. As the minutes crawled by, they became more and more stressed. It was not only tiring going through the scrolls one by one, but it was also disheartening each time one of the twins unfurled yet another page of unhelpful material. So far, they had learned what the current emperor ate each night (he did eat a large amount of mushrooms, Yun noted), the names of his favorite officials, the amount of silk slippers the empress purchased and what colors they came in (492, and mostly red), and the number of dumplings made from the Tang Dynasty up until then.

After an hour or so, Yun put back the scroll he was reading. His eyes were bloodshot as he glanced at the rest of the massive library. "This search could go on for a while," he said. "We need help, or we'll be here until dawn and still may not have found anything."

Mei closed the book she was skimming. She knew it was partially her fault—she should've clarified with Princess Zali exactly where the records of arrests were kept—but she refused to admit her mistake in front of her twin.

"We just need to find the section that keeps criminal records," she said. "Think. Aren't you supposedly good at puzzles?"

The words were bait, and both twins knew it. Yun, like his sister, could never turn down a challenge when it played to his strengths.

He looked around the gigantic space and, for the first time, really thought about it. Where would he keep such sensitive records, if he were the emperor? Certainly not near the front. No, he'd keep those in the back, where they were less likely to be swiped. He followed his instincts and kept walking. Mei trailed behind skeptically.

The room grew dimmer the farther they went. Then a soft,

white glow caught their eye beyond several tall bookshelves. They followed the light until they stood before an enormous stone display case. Inside was a single, wooden box, carved with crisscrossed patterns and tiny windows so that they could see the inside, which was full of floating white-and-black spheres the size of cherries. There were about a dozen or so, drifting slowly like fireflies at night, rotating so that the twins would first see the black half, then the white half. The thick stone case protecting the box and the orbs looked unbreakable. No doubt these were some of the most heavily guarded treasures in the palace.

"What *are* those?" said Mei.

"I'm not sure," answered Yun, staring at the floating orbs.

Beneath the cage was a shiny scroll. They read the inscription.

Yin and yang.
These ancient relics have been preserved since the
    beginning of time.
May the two worlds combine and live in harmony.

They watched the orbs for several moments, entranced by their soft glow. Then Yun's gaze fell on the wall of closed cabinets behind the display case. Five locked chests lined the bottom. To the left of the chests was a row of books with dark blue bindings.

He grabbed a book from the shelf. There they were: records of arrests—thousands upon thousands throughout history, arranged by name of city.

"City of Ashes...City of Ashes..." Yun searched the pages under the light of the floating orbs, tried the next book, then the next.

"The city wasn't always ashes," said Mei. "Before Lotus's curse, I mean. I bet it had a different name." She squeezed her eyes shut. "What do you think it was? City of Walls? City of Mountains?"

"Well, not walls," said Yun. "Because those were built later to keep in Lotus and her magic. But you're right, it did have a different name. I know we've heard it before."

Together, they called to mind the stories Grandpa had told them, and what they'd seen themselves in the City of Ashes. They thought of the Temple of Fire, and the paintings Lotus had looked upon with longing on its walls. And that's when Yun remembered.

"Blossoms," he whispered. "It was called the City of Blossoms."

Mei grinned, and Yun did, too. He hurriedly studied the book in his hand. A moment later, he flipped to a page and pointed to it excitedly. "Here! A list of crimes recorded for the City of Blossoms. Theft of a paintbrush, theft of calligraphy ink, family dispute, vandalism, another theft..." He squinted at the characters. "Wow, so many of these thefts involve stolen art supplies. The city must've had a ton of artists."

"Just like Grandpa said." Mei joined her brother and read over his shoulder. "Skip to the last ones," she said. "The city fell right after Lotus's husband was arrested and killed."

Yun turned the page and read the last entry.

Year of the Horse, 4160. Third full moon. Gardener Wong (see entry 43) arrested on suspicion of treason. On gardener's property, the Noble General discovered letters plotting to assassinate the Emperor of China, as well as poisonous herbs. Evidence in Chest 3, Section 10. Wife, city poet known as Lotus, tried to appeal on husband's behalf.

Verdict: Guilty. Executed in the pre-dawn hours the day following his arrest.

"Chest three," murmured Mei.

She went over to the row of chests and tried to open the third one. It wouldn't budge.

"I know, I know," she said before Yun could say anything. She reached into her hair and tossed the butterfly pin to him. Yun started picking at the lock like he'd done earlier with the empress's door. The chest remained shut.

"That's no ordinary keyhole," Yun said after several long minutes. He studied the tiny engravings on the lock—he could just make out the imprint of a dragon. "I bet the emperor has a special key for this. We need something bigger and sharper than this pin. A tool, like a knife."

Mei looked around the room. There were only fragile scrolls and books. "Maybe we can break it open," she suggested.

"With what?" The wood looked ten times heavier than the firewood the village boys carried home.

Mei's gaze fell on one of the many lanterns along the walls. "We can burn it open."

"And risk burning all the evidence inside?"

The twins tinkered with the chest for a half hour more. Finally, Yun let out an annoyed sigh and sat back in frustration. "It's no use," he grumbled, kicking the chest. "We were so close!" His head ached with sleep, and he shook it side to side to stay awake.

Mei, too, was exhausted. "We're giving up?" she said bitterly. "After everything?"

"There's nothing we can do," replied Yun wearily.

"What about everyone trapped in the City of Ashes? What about our *parents*?" Mei felt her chin quiver, and she clenched her jaw tighter. "If we can't do it, then we'll go straight to the Emperor of China. We'll ask *him* to open the chests."

"That won't work and you know it."

It was a slap in the twins' faces to have come so far, yet still be so distant from their goal. They sat for several long moments, deeply fatigued. The air around them was hot and stuffy, and the City of Ashes flashed through their minds: the desolate streets, the abandoned buildings. Grandpa's steady denials of the rumors, and how the twins' illusion of safety shattered when the truth started trickling through like the leak in the ceiling of their washroom whenever it rained. Mei, who didn't know which side to believe; Yun, who believed every side.

Abruptly, they felt the floor rumble. The air felt warm, like there was a hearth nearby and someone had left live coals inside.

"It's an earthquake," gasped Yun.

"No, look, it's coming from there!" Mei pointed.

The glowing orbs in the display case had grown brighter,

the dancing spheres moving faster and faster. They began to collide with one another. When they did, the spheres fell apart and became two separate orbs, one black, one white. They multiplied inside the wooden box until they threatened to burst out.

Shadows danced across the twins' faces. Suddenly, all the chests started shaking, too. Yun jumped back; the lock was hot.

"What's happening?" shouted Mei above the rumbling.

A series of *clicks* echoed around the library. Scrolls fluttered on shelves. Books shifted. The twins ducked their heads and crouched for cover. There was a flash of white light.

Then the air cooled again, and all became still. The orbs had fused back into white-and-black spheres. Next to them, a thin, glowing white fog rippled through the air like smoke in the wind.

Carefully, Yun examined the chest before them again. The top creaked open.

The twins stared wordlessly at each other, then inside the chest. The contents were organized into neat bins—evidence for miscellaneous crimes. There were calligraphy brushes, old shoes, bloodstained weapons, incriminating notes. Mei and Yun felt queasy as they carefully searched the contents under the label for Section Ten.

"I'm guessing it's these." Yun held up a stack of letters and several small satchels of pale green, bitter-smelling leaves. "Let's hurry. I want to get out of this magical library as fast as possible, before something else happens."

Together, they silently read the letters one by one. The eloquent letters, beautifully scripted and addressed to an unknown recipient, detailed the gardener's hatred for the emperor for marrying the woman he wanted. Outlined in the letters was a vile assassination plot, a sinister plan requiring knowledge of poisonous herbs and toxic flower stems.

"It doesn't make sense," Yun said, breaking the silence. "From what Lotus described, she and her husband were madly in love. Why would he try to assassinate the emperor over another woman?"

"Love isn't always straightforward, obviously," said Mei, who thought herself somewhat of an expert on heartbreak, after a boy she'd liked in the village had called her a skinny monkey for climbing too many trees. (The boy's front porch had mysteriously been piled with dirt and branches for the next week; they never caught the culprit.) "But if Lotus says her husband was framed, someone else must have written these letters."

They reread the letters again. Then Yun looked up with an odd expression.

"These are very well-written, wouldn't you say?" he said. "Not a single grammar or spelling error."

"Yes, so?"

"How could he be the author? He was just a simple gardener."

"*We're* just simple villagers—'peasants,'" Mei reminded her brother. "And we know how to read and write just as well as anyone in the fancy cities."

"You're right. It's just...some of this word usage is so elevated and elaborate." Yun pointed to one of the letters. "Like saying *exempt from burdensome complications* when the word *easy* would do."

He grabbed the blue book and flipped through the entries. He studied the pages; his eyes widened. "Look where it says *'see entry 43,'* next to the gardener's name. Here's the entry in question."

Year of the Snake, 4159. Fifth new moon. Verbal dispute between Gardener Wong and the Noble General. Latter stepped into a row of freshly planted manure because of miswritten sign:

小星

"Little star," Yun said, pointing to the characters. "It's a homonym with the phrase *be cautious.*"

"You're right," answered Mei excitedly. Misusing written characters was common for those who weren't familiar with the subtle differences. "Like mixing the character for *ten*"—she traced a 十 symbol—"with the character for *stone.*" Mei traced a 石 symbol. "But words like *little star* and *be cautious*...those are elementary. If the gardener misspelled even those, then..."

"Then it's *very* unlikely he could have written these long, eloquent letters!" said Yun breathlessly.

Mei gasped as another thought hit her. "Remember what Lotus said? She'd recite her poetry out loud to her husband because *he wasn't the best reader.* He couldn't read well!"

Yun held up the bundle of papers. "It's close, but it's not ideal evidence. The gardener could have asked someone to transcribe the letters for him, for instance. And another question—what about these toxic herbs?"

Mei took the blue book. "I bet we can find more evidence in these other entries. Let's read through these carefully."

Their spirits rising, they read the entries one by one. Fifteen entries later, one in particular caught their eye.

Year of the Horse, 4160. Third new moon. Apothecary broken into at night. Missing potions and herbs. Amount insignificant for compensation.

"The break-in happened the exact same month Lotus's husband was framed," pointed out Yun. "Look, 'missing potions and herbs.' " He glanced at Mei in astonishment. "Do you know what this means?"

"Way ahead of you. Let's get out of here."

They gathered the letters and the blue book excitedly. Their next steps were still a blur, but they would figure them out later. They made their way to the front of the library and exited the doors with their haul. As they shut the door, they realized with surprise that it was daytime.

Then they looked more closely at the orange skies, the hazy courtyard.

"Uh...Mei? Are you seeing what I'm seeing?"

"We're in a dream?" Mei whispered. "But...how? When did it happen?"

They ran through the yard, trying to find someone, anyone. A lone individual was walking across the courtyard. Their features were blurry, as if the twins were viewing the person from underwater. But when they moved closer, Mei recognized something familiar about the figure.

"You were in the audience during the play!" she gasped.

The figure faced them and spoke. "Hey, it's those terrible actors!" And then, turning specifically to Yun, the figure added, "Statues don't move, stupid."

Yun whirled to face Mei. "What's *happening*?"

"I don't know!" answered Mei, equally bewildered. "What should we do?"

The courtyard began to shimmer, and the daylight began to fade. Next thing the twins knew, they were lying on cold, damp stone. Their feet and hands were chained. As their eyes adjusted to the darkness, a familiar voice said gleefully behind them, "The question is, What should *I* do with troublemaking thieves like you?"

It was Fu-Fu.

CHAPTER EIGHTEEN

十八

Connections

The boy looked quite pleased with himself as he watched the twins from outside the iron bars that imprisoned them. A dim candle lit the dungeon hall. Somewhere, a steady drip-drop of water leaked from the ceiling. Mei and Yun glanced at each other. They had the uneasy feeling that nothing was quite real anymore.

"You're in big trouble," Fu-Fu said in a singsong voice. "You're not allowed in the Imperial Library."

"What happened?" cried Mei. "Tell us what happened right now!"

Fu-Fu clutched his bamboo stick and pointed it at the twins. "I found you all by myself. I saw you talking with Cousin Zali earlier and knew something was fishy. So I followed you from the rooftops. I can't believe you were dumb enough to break into the enchanted library."

Mei moved her right hand and noticed the seal was no longer in her palm. Fu-Fu held up the gleaming square. "Looking for this?" he taunted. He lowered his voice. "The guards didn't even notice when I swiped it from you. What idiots."

"What guards?" said Yun.

"The ones who arrested you in the library when you two were asleep. *I* called for them, by the way. Nobody's supposed to be in the library. That's a rule even I don't break, mostly because books and scrolls are boring. What kind of thieves are you anyway, falling *asleep* on the job?"

"But we weren't asleep," Yun said, looking from Fu-Fu to his sister. He started to chew his fingernails, but his hands were tied. "Right?"

"Yes, you were." Fu-Fu gleefully told them how normally, any intruders would be killed on the spot, but then Fu-Fu had argued on the twins' behalf. "I told them to toss you in the dungeon for now, and not to bother the emperor at this late an hour. They're finishing their card game right now." He glanced at Mei. "You can thank me anytime."

"But—but—" Yun halted. The blue book and letters were gone, too.

"How is this possible?" exclaimed Mei.

"You can stop performing now," Fu-Fu sneered. "You're the worst actors of this *dynasty*."

Yun imagined Fu-Fu's smug face in place of the fish Chef Fan had smacked a few days earlier. He took a deep breath and addressed the young master, his voice shaking, "Look, we do not want to cause any harm. We needed to prove someone in a city near our village was framed for a crime seventy years ago. Our village has been cursed as a result, and our grandpa's been arrested—" Yun shook his head again, interrupting his usual longwinded explanations. "You know what? Forget it. You wouldn't understand anyway."

"There's been a mistake," said Mei. "Have someone call for Princess Zali."

Something had suddenly changed in Fu-Fu's demeanor. He pointed at them with the sharp stick. "Tell me the whole story about this cursed village," he ordered. There was a long pause. "Or I'll call the guards, and *not* summon the princess," he added, narrowing his eyes.

Seeing no other option, Yun and Mei stiffly explained the City of Ashes, how a poet had cursed the city after the Noble General framed her beau, how the letters had been forged, and how the accused party was semi-illiterate.

"It's nothing of interest to you," Yun finished. "I told you so."

But Fu-Fu was now staring at them with an odd expression. His face darkened.

"This Noble General," he said slowly. "You're saying *he* was the one who wrote the letters that wrongly sentenced a man to death?"

"We think so," said Mei. "He's the one who supposedly found the so-called evidence. Planted it himself, most likely. It's all there in the library."

"What were *you* two going to do with this information?"

"We haven't worked out the details yet," Yun said impatiently. "Show the evidence to the authorities, probably."

Fu-Fu glowered at them. His hand gripped his bamboo

stick so tight, his knuckles were white. "Why are you trying to clear some dead guy's name?"

"We told you. An entire city, including our village, has been cursed. We've been asked to clear his name so things can go back to normal."

"The fates of many people rest on our success," said Mei. "You don't want peoples' lives on your conscience, do you? Oh, wait," she couldn't help adding sourly, "I bet you don't even know what conscience *means*."

Mei's remark was the one to finally break Fu-Fu's restraint. "I'm not *stupid*!" he roared, making Mei and Yun jump back in alarm. "I'm just as clever as Cousin Zali!" the boy continued angrily. "I read as much as she does. I'm better at archery and combat than most of my cousins. But no one ever praises *me*. Do you know why? It's because I'm not a prince, that's why!"

"We're not from royalty, either," Mei quickly soothed, trying to get the boy to quiet down so others wouldn't hear. "We're from a poor village in the mountains."

"I said I wasn't a *prince*—I didn't say I was a dirty peasant like you," Fu-Fu retorted.

Mei's face hardened. "Oh, well, *that's* good to know."

Fu-Fu stamped his foot and thumped his bamboo stick hard on the ground. "I'm not much different from the royal family. I've had tea with the empress, and she says I have fine etiquette. My tutor says I'm clever. He says my penmanship is excellent. The other kids think they're better than me because I'm not descended from a long line of royalty." The boy glared at them, as if daring the twins to disagree. "I'm just as valuable."

"You *are* valuable," said Yun in his most ingratiating

voice, lying through his teeth. "You are excellent and great and marvelous. You'll be even more marvelous if you help us."

"Come on," pleaded Mei. "If you help us rescue our village, you'll be a hero. Maybe they'll raise a statue in your honor."

"Or something of the kind," muttered Yun, thinking a statue was going too far.

Fu-Fu stuck out his chin. "I'll never help you. The story is a dirty lie!" He stamped his foot again. "You're liars. Liars, liars, *LIARS!*"

His shouting had alerted the guards. Five seconds later, servants and guards scurried into the corridor. "Halt, stay away from the young master!" they hollered to the twins. Some of the guards drew their swords.

"Look, now you can engage in a real sword fight," Fu-Fu said with a smirk.

"What's *wrong* with you?" Mei gripped the bars and shook them angrily.

"Why are you doing this?" sighed an equally weary Yun.

The small boy didn't flinch. "Because," he said simply, "my great-grandfather was the Noble General."

CHAPTER NINETEEN

十九

Dice of Destiny

The palace's prison guards were perplexed that night. It still confused them how the two siblings managed to break into the Imperial Library. They argued amongst themselves for a bit, then finally decided to blame the oversight on Xia, an unlikable colleague whom they nicknamed "The Crane" and who (coincidentally) had won last night's card game.

They were also struggling over what to do with the twins. Although Mei and Yun seemed harmless and likely didn't pose a serious danger to the palace, the fact that they'd been found inside the sealed library was definitely incriminating—and, like Master Fu-Fu had reminded them, embarrassing. Merely locking the twins up for the night was insufficient. The guards debated heatedly among themselves over what to do as they gathered outside the twins' cell.

"Just slit their throats and dump their bodies in the trash!" "No, bring them to the emperor." "Nonsense! The emperor would think we're incompetent if we couldn't even stop a pair of children." "Have them pay us money." "Are you kidding? These commoners look poorer than rats in trash."

Finally, the head guard decided, "We shall kill them and get it over with."

"Hold up!" interrupted Fu-Fu. "*I'm* the one who caught them. I should get to pick the punishment."

"I do not think that is necessary," the guard replied dismissively. "Why don't you run along and leave the punishing to the experts."

"They're my age, so I know *exactly* the thing to make them wet their pants. Besides, remember who you're talking to." Fu-Fu held up his stick menacingly.

There was a pause. The twins, who stood trembling behind the bars, didn't think the guards were *actually* afraid of Fu-Fu, but also guessed the guards didn't want to deal with his tantrums. Either way, punishment to the point of pants-wetting was far preferable to being run through with a broadsword, so the twins hoped the guards would listen to the little brat... even if he did happen to be the great-grandson of a notorious murderer.

"Very well," the head guard said. "What do you suggest, Master Fu-Fu?"

There was no smile on Fu-Fu's face as his gaze fell on the twins. "I suggest imprisoning them for a day and feeding them nothing but vinegar and hot chili peppers."

"They're trespassers and thieves. Mere imprisonment is insufficient."

Fu-Fu glanced at Mei again, then back at the guards. "How about flogging one of them? I suggest the boy."

"Just go ahead and kill them!" a brutish guard in the back called. The others muttered in agreement.

"Or—or make them play Dice of Destiny!" Fu-Fu hurried to say.

Several guards nodded, murmuring, "Good idea, let luck decide." The head guard mulled over it for a bit longer. Finally, he agreed.

Minutes later, the twins found themselves being dragged along the corridor while Fu-Fu hurried quietly alongside them. "No, please take us to Princess Zali," Mei begged of the guard gripping her upper arm. "We were only running an errand for Her Highness. Ask her!"

Predictably, the guards ignored her. Next to Mei, Yun, who had concluded such appeals would be worthless, whispered, "The princess can only stick her neck out for us so far. Logically, she'll deny her role in this. We have to face facts: we're going to die!"

Maybe this is also a dream, Mei wanted to say. But instead, she turned to Fu-Fu and asked, "What's Dice of Destiny?"

"You'll see," he replied.

The guards escorted the twins around a corner and to a heavy-looking door at the end of another hall. A stony-faced man stood in front of it. "Trespassers and thieves," the head guard announced. He thrust Mei and Yun forward. "Young Master Fu-Fu here has suggested Dice of Destiny as punishment."

With a silent nod, the man guarding the door stepped aside. Mei and Yun followed the guards past him.

"Where are we?" Mei whispered to Yun, wishing she had Princess Zali's map of the Imperial City in front of her.

"Based on my recollections of the palace layout, I believe we're in the guards' quarters," Yun murmured back.

They had entered a large room. The twins blinked to adjust their eyes to the sudden light and din that surrounded them. The room was actually a large hall with rows of tables, each one piled with cards or game boards. Groups of five or six men were gathered at each table, laughing and chatting animatedly, or else scowling and serious.

The guards took the twins to a dimmer section toward the back, where a small table sat in a pool of moonlight streaming through a nearby window. The table was bare, save for a pair of dice and an empty bowl.

Several members of the crowd, who had curiously watched them pass, now clamored around the table, murmuring with anticipation.

"It's—it's a game?" asked Yun, his eyes wide.

"Kind of," said the guard to his left. "It's a rather benevolent punishment, all things considered." His companions barked in laughter.

The head guard silenced the audience, then announced, "Judgment is ripe upon these prisoners. Today's crime: breaking and entering!"

"And thievery," someone else called.

"A crime worthy of the dice!"

The audience cheered and called out bets on what was about to unfold. The head guard faced upward and recited,

"Dice of destiny seal your fate,
Cast fair and foul upon this date.
All pairs fickle and bear suspense,
Luck alone is your defense.
But mind the pair that steals your breath:
The lowest roll will bring forth death."

"Did he say *death*?" whispered Mei. In the crowd, Fu-Fu suddenly looked pale.

The guard told Mei and Yun the rules. "The prisoner starts with a score of zero and must roll the dice three times. If the sum of the amounts on the dice is an even number, that number is added to the prisoner's score. If the sum is an odd number, that number is subtracted. If both dice show the same number, then the score resets to zero. At the end of the three rolls, the prisoner needs an overall number above zero if he or she wants to live."

Yun had never heard of a more atrocious game. "This is ridiculous!" he sputtered.

"One more thing. The prisoner needs to avoid rolling two ones—also known as 'snake eyes.' If you do, then the game is automatically over, and you lose. Well? Are you ready to play?"

Mei and Yun trembled. In the crowd, Fu-Fu called out, "Hold on, I thought if they lose, they get imprisoned in the dungeon for a month."

"No, *Master* Fu-Fu," said the head guard tonelessly; *you annoying git* seemed implied, though never spoken. "Losing in Dice of Destiny always means death."

"W-Well, there are two of them," argued Fu-Fu. "Why

don't you just take one of them as the prisoner who plays and release the other one?"

The crowd murmured. The head guard seemed to consider this. As he did so, the twins glanced at each other.

"This was my fault, Yun," blurted Mei, her chin quivering. She held her head high, as she refused to cry in front of the guards, especially the rotten Fu-Fu. "I'll play. You can go. You'll find a way to save Grandpa and the village, I know you will."

Next to her, Yun fervently shook his head. "No, if you're playing, then I'm playing. We're a team." He turned to address the head guard. "In fact, Mei and I should count as one prisoner."

He had calculated the odds in his head. It was more favorable for both of them if they only needed to beat the odds once.

The head guard hesitated, then said, "Fine."

Mei nudged her brother. "Do you know what you're doing?" she whispered.

Yun nodded, though he was still trembling.

"It's fine," he reassured her. "Even if all doesn't . . ." He tried again. "Even if things don't go as planned, we tried. That's what's important, right?"

Mei nodded slowly. This they agreed upon, absolutely. At least afterward, people would say, *Ah, yes, the odd but commendable Wu twins died while trying to save their village.*

"Let the game . . . begin!" announced the head guard.

The room fell silent. Yun slowly picked up the pair of dice, shook them, then dropped them in the bowl.

"Four, five," read the guard. "Score: negative nine."

The crowd oohed. "Better write up an epitaph," someone called.

Yun's mind raced. There was a 50 percent chance they'd roll another odd number—the same as flipping a coin—and then no amount would bring them back to the positive side. There was a 33 percent chance they'd roll an even number, an even smaller chance they'd roll a zero, and a sliver of a chance that they'd roll snake eyes. His head ached from the calculations.

"Let me do it," said Mei in a hoarse voice, her skin prickling. "I have a good feeling."

Yun stared at his sister. *Ridiculous,* he was about to say, but then he paused. For the first time, he understood a little of what Mei meant when she talked about luck and gut instinct. Even when he had all the calculations laid out in front of him like a map, life still presented opportunities for leaps of faith. He had no good feelings about this whatsoever. But if Mei did...

"Hurry up!" one of the spectators yelled.

Yun handed the dice over to his sister and squeezed her hand. "Good luck," he said, ignoring the somersaults in his stomach.

Mei shakily took the pair of dice, then rolled them into the bowl.

"Four, four," read the guard. "Score: zero."

Groans and boos filled the room. The twins breathed a sigh of relief. Now all they needed to roll was a four, a six, an eight, or a ten. The chance of winning was still not in their favor, but at least they had a shot.

"Last roll!" announced the guard.

The entire room waited. All eyes were on Mei and Yun.

"Want to roll the last one together?" asked Yun with a faint smile.

Mei grinned back nervously and nodded.

They each gripped a die, closed their eyes, then let the dice fall to the bowl. The moonlight shimmered.

There was a deafening silence.

"Three, one," the guard read. "Score: four. The prisoners...are free!"

Half the crowd left in disappointment, but the other half cheered enthusiastically. They clapped the twins' backs, shouting, "Good job!" and "Luck knows no bounds, eh?"

Mei smiled back, accepting the congratulations. She searched the crowd to find Fu-Fu's reaction, but the boy had disappeared.

Yun, meanwhile, was still looking at the table in stunned silence. He stared for a long time at the pair of dice in the bowl, then out the window at the crescent moon. When Mei rejoined him, she followed Yun's gaze. The twins turned to each other with the same question in their eyes.

Even years later, the two siblings never did determine if they had been extraordinary lucky that night, or if they'd gotten a little extra help. As the guards escorted them across the grounds to the palace exits, the twins thought of a story Grandpa told them when they were younger.

Once upon a time, there was a Chinese farmer whose horse ran away. All his neighbors muttered it was bad luck. The farmer replied, "Good luck, bad luck, who can tell?"

The next day, the horse returned and brought seven wild horses with it. All the neighbors came around to congratulate on the farmer's good fortune. The farmer replied, "Good luck, bad luck, who can tell?"

A few days later, one of the farmer's sons tried to ride one of the horses, and he was thrown off and broke his leg. The neighbors agreed amongst themselves that the farmer's life was cursed with misfortune. The farmer replied, "Good luck, bad luck, who can tell?"

Then the next morning, the conscription officers came from the imperial courts to draft young men into the army. They rejected the farmer's son due to his broken leg. Later, all the men in the village who'd been drafted had died in battle. And the neighbors whispered about the farmer's exceeding good luck in life, unparalleled by any. To which the farmer replied, "Good luck, bad luck, who can tell?"

For centuries, hundreds of thousands of humans have tried to understand and control luck, through myriad and odd ways: a bowl of goldfish, a four-leaf clover necklace, or (yes, horrifyingly) a rabbit's foot. Years afterward, Mei and Yun often wondered whether it was bad luck their father had been a scholar, and as a result took their mother to the City of Ashes in the pursuit of knowledge. They wondered whether it was good luck they encountered Princess Zali in the Imperial City, and, yes, even Fu-Fu, who did not turn them in right away.

From my thousands of years' of observation, fortune and

misfortune are misnomers. There are only a series of conse-
quences as life rolls on.

But as for a simple pair of dice rolling to display the exact
numbers one needs to win a game of life and death in the den
of the Imperial Palace? Yun was right to wonder. Sometimes a
little moonlight does the trick.

CHAPTER TWENTY

二十

The Dream World

The guards brought the prisoners to the entrance of the Imperial City. Its large gray doors were as tall and thick as trees. The guards thrust the twins through them and out into the road beyond. As Mei and Yun struggled to their feet, the tall doors slammed shut behind them. They'd been thrown out of the palace.

For several long moments, neither twin spoke as they faced the formidable red walls surrounding the complex. They stood silently in the cold night, the wind whispering in their ears. Behind them, the streets of the Outer City were quiet, the houses silhouetted against the dark. Soft, colorful mists drifted out the windows of the houses, the silky strands a golden yellow and blue.

"Nobody else can see those," Mei said, finally breaking the silence.

Yun glanced at her, wondering what she was referring to. Mei pointed to the windows.

"Outside our family, I mean. We've seen them our whole lives. The dreams. We can see them just like Grandpa can. Just like Mama could, too."

"I know," said Yun, his teeth chattering from nervousness and the cold. "We never thought it was weird. I suppose things often don't seem as strange when you're younger. We simply thought it was a natural part of the world. And turns out, it is."

Yun's observation was a profound one. Though the twins didn't know it at the time, young children often have more pure inquisitiveness than adults, more courage, and more acceptance, too. You can tell kids frightening tales of ferocious beasts who eat peoples' heads, and they'd curiously ask for more. Meanwhile, an adult would immediately claim it's nonsense and insist they have no time for make-believe. Indeed, the bravest adults are often the ones who retain their childlike wonder of the world and are not afraid to consider the unknown or its possibilities.

"The Jade Rabbit's instincts were right, then," said Yun slowly. "We have this ability, to—to see dreams, and the Jade Rabbit said we share the same...*essence* as Lotus's lost city. If that's true, we must have gotten it from Mama, who got hers from Grandpa. Who presumably got his ability from *his* parents. But none of this explains what happened inside the library. I don't even remember falling asleep."

"Me neither. We were really tired, but everything seemed normal." Mei's eyes grew wide, and her mouth dropped.

"Until . . . until the floating orbs started shaking." She stared at Yun. "That must have been a sign we'd fallen asleep—that we were dreaming, just like when the walls of Lotus's dream chamber came alive!"

"Yes," sighed Yun, remembering the brilliant flash of light. "Somehow I knew those chests opening so easily was too good to be true."

"So we fell asleep," Mei repeated, recalling the scenario in her mind's eye. "We only dreamed we opened the evidence chest and found the letters and herbs."

Yet it had seemed impossibly real. If it had indeed been a dream, it felt like a deliberate one, somehow; not like the whimsical, fragmented dreams they normally had when sleeping.

"The Jade Rabbit did say the dream world is the mirror to the physical world," pointed out Yun.

"Do you think what we saw in the dream, then, is actually inside those chests?" continued Mei excitedly.

"Only one way to find out," said Yun. "We have to get back into the library. The question is, how?"

They studied the map of the city that Princess Zali had drawn. Although she'd marked the little-known passageways within the royal city, there was only one entryway to the complex itself, and that was heavily guarded. The stately walls were also better maintained than the ones surrounding the City of Ashes—there were no convenient holes for the twins to crawl through. It was impossible to get back over the wall without the Jade Rabbit's cloud.

They looked at the sky again, waiting for an answer to appear (hopefully in the form of the Jade Rabbit). Unfortunately, life has a rude habit of not always quite granting us the things we want at the moment, whether it's an enormous piece of candy that never shrinks, or a convenient cloud that magically transports its users over walls and across the country.

"I've got an idea," Yun said suddenly.

"What is it?"

"Not a lot of people know about this. The chefs have a secret passageway that leads to the outside. I've never actually used it, but I know the exit is somewhere in the marketplace."

"Yun, that's brilliant!"

They hurried along the Outer City, which had started to wake up for the day. Somewhere, a rooster crowed. Early risers grabbed a change of laundry from clotheslines. A mother rocked her baby to sleep on a porch step while two old men set up a game of chess beside her. It wasn't that much different from the twins' village. They even passed an elderly woman who looked like the female version of Elder Liu.

The marketplace was full of vendors setting up their stalls for the day. The smells of ripe fruits, pork buns, and other foods made the twins' mouths water.

"Breakfast would be nice," Mei said, her stomach growling. Unfortunately, they did not have a single coin in their pockets.

"Once we get back in, we'll have all the breakfast we need," Yun reassured her, thinking of the always-stocked imperial kitchen.

They shuffled through the street, looking for signs of hidden doors or passageways. A few adults frowned at them as they passed. "Looks like a pair of peasants," one of them muttered. Another snorted, "Lazy beggars!"

The twins shrank back in embarrassment. With their dirt-streaked skin and lack of belongings, they really did seem like beggars. Mei was sorely tempted to tell these people that not less than twenty-four hours ago, she'd earned the respect of a real princess, but Yun nudged her and said wisely, "Let it go."

By midday, they'd still had zero success in finding the purported passageway. The sky had become overcast with rolling gray clouds. By early afternoon, the people in the marketplace and the surrounding buildings were in a foul mood. Neighbors argued loudly. Food vendors fought each other, pushing over stands and stomping on each other's fruits and vegetables. The clouds continued to roll overhead, a sheet of white-gray.

Mei and Yun stayed out of everyone's way. They sat in the shadows of a dark alley, keeping an eye on the marketplace for palace chefs and taking turns trying to fall asleep to conserve their energy. But trying to sleep during the day was hard, and doubly so with the rising commotion.

"We'll probably have better luck watching this place at night, when it's deserted," admitted Yun. "We might have to wait a while."

"What's one more day?" agreed Mei wearily.

Someone threw a potted plant out a third-story window. It landed with a clattering crash next to the twins, making them jump. That was when they noticed that the clouds overhead had a vaguely familiar look. They rolled like liquid, and the place suddenly felt extra cold.

"I don't think we have much time left, actually," Mei whispered. "It looks like..."

"...the curse is coming here," finished Yun.

CHAPTER TWENTY-ONE

二十一

The Curse Reborn

Yun bit his fingernails as he pondered the weather. "It must be following the emperor's son on his way back here. This is *not* good."

Mei felt like crying. She thought of the villagers back home and how they had treated one another. If the officials in the Imperial City got affected by the curse, Grandpa was a goner for sure.

And what if the curse afflicted the palace the same way it did the City of Ashes? The twins thought of their parents, forever frozen in time in the forlorn city. They recalled their smiling faces, how Baba always insisted they eat more green vegetables, how Mama sang to Smelly Tail in the kitchen on warm nights.

"There's definitely no other way inside?" asked Mei, her voice higher than usual. "No way at all?"

Yun closed his eyes. "No. It's heavily guarded."

"We have to warn the emperor about the curse. Princess Zali would know what to do. I wish we could ask her."

"Maybe we can." Yun suddenly jumped up and began pacing the alley excitedly.

"What do you mean? How?"

Yun crouched down and lowered his voice. "Maybe we can enter the *dream* world and talk to her."

Mei blinked. "You're thinking . . . we should try to communicate with someone inside the palace . . . *inside our dreams?*"

"Exactly." Yun's mind raced. "The same way we talked to each other a few nights ago, and again last night in the Imperial Library. The Jade Rabbit said dreamweavers have the ability to control all aspects of a dream, even from within. So we just need to dream of finding the princess and communicating with her, the way we did with each other."

"What do you mean, *just?*" asked Mei, her skepticism making her sound like her twin. "How do we control in advance what we dream about?"

"I don't know. It's just a theory, really. But if we truly are dreamweavers, we should be able to work with and *within* dreams . . . right?"

"I don't know what we *should* be able to do. All I know is that Grandpa arrives in one day."

For a moment, Yun was at a loss for words as he tried to describe what he was trying to say. Then he stood and smiled. "Well, if we've got nothing else, then maybe we can go with my gut feeling on this."

Mei looked at him for a few moments. Then she slowly nodded. "All right. But where do we start? Do I just *dream* of walking into the palace and finding Princess Zali in the maze of halls?"

"Ideally, yes. But I'm thinking maybe we have to prepare our minds somehow. Let's think about the palace layout the best we can, so that it's fresh in our heads when we fall asleep. And I assume we need to recreate the exact conditions, sleeping patterns...." Yun first lay on his right side, then on his left. "Let's see...that night, Chef Fan's snores had woken me up, so I turned this way, and my neck was turned at a slight angle...."

Mei yawned, then wrinkled her eyebrows. "What are you doing?"

"I'm trying to retrace my exact movements from the first night we were able to communicate in our dreams."

Renewed by this bizarre idea, the twins tried their best to relax, hoping to recreate what had occurred before. It took a while before they could fall asleep, partly because of the wind, partly because of their nervousness.

But when they opened their eyes again, they were lying in the same alleyway. The only thing that had changed was that it was early evening.

"What did you dream of?" asked Mei.

"Food," Yun grumbled. He slumped his shoulders in defeat. "I don't know what we're doing wrong. I'm detailing everything the best I can in my head, like where the guards are and how to get past the walls, and going through the different quarters...."

"We didn't worry about those things when we went to see Lotus," Mei said slowly. "We sort of wished to see her, or *wanted* to...and then she appeared in her dream chamber."

"That's right," Yun said, sitting up straight. "When we first communicated in our dreams that first night, we didn't think about the hows. We just knew we wanted to talk to each other after so many days of being apart."

"Same thing happened in the library," added Mei. "We wanted to open the chests, and...they opened."

"That's the key, then!" said Yun. "It's like what the Jade Rabbit told us! In the physical world, we think of how to get from step one to step two. In the dream world, step two comes to you because you wish for it."

"Provided they make their wishes clear..." said Mei, remembering the creature's words. In spite of the evidence, she still couldn't help feeling dubious. "So you're saying we should just *wish* for Princess Zali to appear before we fall asleep?"

"That's the plan."

☀

Meanwhile, on the other side of the palace walls, the Imperial City was in mild chaos. The palace infirmary was bustling with patients brought quietly but urgently to the nurses and physicians.

"We've got another one," a servant called as he carried one of the royal members inside.

A physician leaned over to examine the young girl. "What is your age?"

The girl hiccupped, then said,

"I come before seven,
Arrive after five.
These are the number of
Years I've been alive."

The physician looked grave. "This is serious. How long has she been speaking like this?"

"She started just today," the servant answered. "It comes and goes."

Behind them in the infirmary, a few dozen more patients were mumbling worriedly. None of them seemed able to speak a proper sentence. Instead, every statement came in the form of an elaborate riddle.

"No, no!" one of the patients, a high official, said to the nurse. "I said to get me a"—he hiccupped, then continued— "that which cleans but gets dirtier with time!"

"I'm sorry, sir, I don't know what the answer is!" his nurse answered fretfully.

"That which cleans but gets dirtier with time!" the official repeated, pointing to his lips. "Once pristine but accumulates grime!"

"I've got it!" someone else said. "He wants a rag."

On the other side of the infirmary, a nine-year-old boy was swinging his bamboo stick moodily as the physicians tended to him. He kept saying angrily,

"The truth resides within the double,
The pair that caused infinite trouble!"

The physicians had never seen such a thing. They tried feeding the patients herbal teas and bitter medicines. They placed cold rags on their heads. They even tried taping one patient's mouth shut. More and more patients showed up throughout the day.

Then one physician remembered something. He hurried to the bookshelf, where hundreds of scrolls and binders were kept.

"My father mentioned an unusual case from when he worked here," he said. "I recall it was similar...." The physician grabbed one of the archived scrolls and unraveled it. "Aha!" he said, pointing to the scroll. His look of triumph turned to worry.

"What is it?" the others asked.

"Almost seventy years ago, a general was afflicted with a frightening speech impediment. He could only speak in riddles."

"Yes," said the servant with the little girl. "That's where that one quote is passed down from: *'Better to be a salamander than to be a babbling commander.'* What's the pattern? Who's being affected?"

"We're not sure yet," the physician responded. "We're trying to ask the patients questions, but it's difficult to get a straight answer." He put the scroll back and looked out the window at the rolling clouds, something the palace meteorologists had never seen before, either. "But whatever afflicted the babbling commander is back."

✳

That night, Princess Zali concentrated at the parchment on her writing desk. Her latest invention was a comb made of razors, but she was having problems with the design.

"The razor must be able to embed itself in the skin *deep* enough," she muttered, "while still disguised as a flowery comb."

In frustration, she crumpled up the paper and threw it across the room. She was in a fouler mood than usual. Everything felt rather pointless. Maybe the others were right. Why did *she* think she was good for anything other than to sit and look pretty?

The princess yawned. It was time for bed. Outside, the dreary weather from earlier continued into the night.

A little while after she extinguished the oil lamps, she fell into a familiar dream.

Her brothers stood at the front of an ornate hall. Their backs were turned to the princess, and the emperor—her father—was congratulating each of them. "For your physical strength," he said to one. "For your prowess in battle," he said to another.

What about me? Princess Zali waved for their attention, but they ignored her. She spoke, but their laughter drowned out her voice. The men grew more and more distant, until the figures vanished from the hall completely. The princess now stood in the courtyard, facing the blurry figure of a twelve-year-old girl.

"It's you," Princess Zali said in surprise. She rubbed her eyes. The girl was faded in color, and her face was hard to read. "I've been worried about you."

"Princess Zali?" Mei squeaked. Then, in triumph, "It worked! It *worked*!"

"The plan worked?" repeated the princess. "You were able to rescue your village?"

"Not exactly."

The princess listened as Mei explained how she and her brother broke into the empress's quarters and found the seal, how they went inside the Imperial Library and found the letters, about the glowing orbs. She mentioned Dice of Destiny and how they were thrown out of the palace. With each fantastic story, the scene around them changed in swirls of colors, from the long corridors, to the locked library, to the cell that had held the twins, until Mei and the princess found themselves in the middle of the guards' quarters in the dungeons. They stood facing the long rows of empty tables.

When all was finished, Princess Zali said the only thing it made sense to say. "None of us have ever seen anything glow inside the box."

"Er, pardon?" asked Mei.

"The box in the Imperial Library, the one that holds the Orbs of Opposites. For the longest time, I thought it was just an old, empty box from millenniums past. We all did."

"I'm pretty sure my brother and I can see them because we're dreamweavers. We can move from the physical world to the dream world in a way that we can control...or are learning to control, anyway. In fact, that's how I'm speaking with you right now."

Another shadow materialized in the room. Mei's twin stepped forward, looking stunned.

"Yun, I thought you were keeping a lookout!" said Mei.

"I was tired and fell asleep too, I guess." The newcomer blinked at the princess, then quickly bowed. "Sorry to interrupt, Your Highness."

Mei turned back to the princess. "This is my brother, Yun." There was affection in her voice this time, unlike the icy tone she'd used when she spoke of him after the play.

"Nice to meet you," Princess Zali said. "Mei told me how you broke into Mother's chamber. You must teach me the ways of lock picking," she added, which made Yun blush the color of a ripe plum.

Though the princess still could not make out her expression, Mei's voice grew serious. "Listen, Princess Zali, we don't have much time. It's coming. The curse—it's coming to the palace."

Together, the twins explained the rolling clouds and what they foretold. Princess Zali felt her chest grow tight.

"Impossible," she breathed after the twins finished.

"We swear," said Mei. "Haven't you noticed anything strange in the Imperial City today?"

Princess Zali gave a terse nod. She hadn't left her quarters that day, but she recalled how one of her cousins she passed in the hallway had spoken in rhyme.

"That's why we need to get back in," joined in Yun. "The curse will lift only if we clear Lotus's husband's name. Meanwhile, you need to warn the rest of the palace."

"It will be hard getting members of the royal family on my side," said Princess Zali, whose senses finally seemed to return. "You realize the words of two random children—intruders and thieves, no less—are not going to convince most people? You need to obtain the evidence and show them."

"We don't have the seal anymore," Mei said. "Fu-Fu took it. But maybe you can help us. Everything we need is in the Imperial Library. We can tell you exactly where the evidence is."

Princess Zali pursed her lips. "Again, this is a chicken-and-egg problem. I cannot convince someone to get the evidence without telling them your side of the story. And I cannot tell your side of the story without getting the evidence first. However, if Fu-Fu has the seal..." The princess paused. "You know, Fu-Fu knows more secret passageways than I do, and he's much quicker and stealthier. If there's one thing he likes, it's breaking rules."

"Oh, no," groaned Mei, evidently seeing where this was going. Yun did, too, and said, "There's no way you're suggesting . . . ?"

"Yes. Unfortunately, Fu-Fu is our best bet at this point. You'll have to appeal to him."

Mei and Yun gaped at her. "Appeal to the brat Fu-Fu?" sputtered Yun. "No offense, Your Highness, but he's like, eight years old—"

"Nine and a half," corrected Princess Zali.

"—and he nearly got us killed!"

"Plus he claims he's the Noble General's great-grandson," joined in Mei.

Princess Zali blinked. "That could very well be true. Let me guess: he's upset and won't let you besmirch his great-grandfather's good name?"

The twins nodded. "There's no way we can convince him, but *you* can," said Mei.

Princess Zali looked skeptical. "I have the feeling you wish me to come up with a decree, something like, *I shall force Fu-Fu to replace the stolen seal, by my father's power!*"

"Sure, that sounds good," Yun said quickly.

"If only you knew how little power I have," the princess said wryly. After a few moments, she spoke again. "I understand where Fu-Fu is coming from. Our ancestors are an important part of who we are. More people in this palace likely have relations to the Noble General, not only Fu-Fu."

The hall disappeared, replaced by faded portraits of Princess Zali's cousins and various officials.

"Like...the emperor's son!" said Yun, glancing at one of the faded figures. "The one who came to visit our village."

"Precisely. If the general was already quite unpopular in his day, proof of this frame-up, which inadvertently led to the destruction of an entire city, would make his legacy ten times worse. Nobody wants something like that dug up on their family name. You understand, surely?"

The twins started to protest. The princess pursed her lips and waited for the siblings to calm down. "You will have to find a way to convince Fu-Fu," she repeated. "I am not in the best position to help you. Not with something like this."

"Maybe we can bribe Fu-Fu," suggested Mei after a moment.

"Don't bother. If material wealth was enough to make someone happy, everyone here in the palace would be smiling perpetually. Fu-Fu has never been a happy kid. Even more so now. He's likely going to be afflicted by the babbling curse soon, if he hasn't already."

Mei and Yun were quiet. The princess raised her head.

"Do not be so glum. In one week, you've managed to enter the Imperial City, infiltrate the palace, break into the Imperial Library, and find evidence that clears an innocent person of a crime that was committed seventy years ago. It's clear you two are extraordinary people. I'll..." The princess took a deep breath. "I'll do what I can on my side, arranging things with the emperor for what I expect will be a trial for your grandfather. But the rest falls in your hands."

"We're just a couple of peasants," grumbled Yun.

"The Monkey King was considered to be just a stinky primate by some, yet he was the hero of his story. In the same way, you two are the heroes of your story." The princess smiled. "That I am sure of."

Mei stood straight. "I think I know how to convince Fu-Fu," she said confidently. Before she and Yun vanished, Mei said to the princess, "You are the hero of your own story, too."

Then the twins disappeared. The hall faded back to the princess's quarters. Princess Zali blinked in the dark. She was back in her bed, thoughts swirling in her mind.

She sat up and called for the servants stationed outside her door. They entered the room.

"What is it, Your Highness?" they asked.

"Please send an urgent message to my father," the princess replied. "I wish to request an audience with him."

CHAPTER TWENTY-TWO

二十二

Dreamfishing

Later that same night, after awakening in their hiding place, Mei and Yun finally spotted the hidden trapdoor in the marketplace, next to a furtive vendor selling peacock eggs and other strange delicacies the twins had never tried. They made their way inside the hidden tunnel. The passageway was narrow, the air thin. There was no light at either end, only the faint knowledge inside their hearts that they needed to keep going.

Half an hour later, slightly covered in soot and grime, they finally made their way back to the palace kitchen. It was much quieter at night, no chefs and servants flying about. Outside the tall windows, the bright moon peeked in and out behind the clouds, covering the tables and stoves in the still room with its white light.

Yun handed Mei an apron, then tied an identical one around his waist. "I still don't know your plan for Fu-Fu," he said uneasily. "Shouldn't we be trying to get back into the Imperial Library somehow, ourselves?"

"No, I have a gut feeling about this one," answered Mei. "Trust me."

She searched the kitchen shelves until she spotted the perfect container. She clutched the porcelain box, then motioned for Yun to follow her. They stepped back into the courtyard and headed toward the quarters where the royal family slept. The twins, still in their servant attire, quietly nodded to the guards on duty along the way, many of whom nodded cheerfully back. Mei and Yun glanced at each other. It was lucky for them that the guards were not as good at recognizing people as Princess Zali was.

Finally, they slipped past the corner and stopped near the first-floor windows of the royal residences. The sound of soft snoring reverberated on the other side.

"I don't know about this—" Yun began, but Mei shushed him reassuringly and carefully pushed open the window.

The room was as lavish as Princess Zali's, with rich carpeting and a plush canopy bed. Floating in the middle of the room was a dreamcloud, sunshine yellow like the petals of a chrysanthemum flower. The royal subject, another princess from the looks of it, was deep in sleep and did not hear the twins. It took just a moment after the window was opened for the night breeze to slowly carry the cloud toward Mei and Yun.

Mei readied herself. She gave the lid of the box to Yun, then carefully leaned forward and held it under the floating cloud. With her other hand, she gingerly waved the air, fanning the dreamcloud inch by inch inside the box, the threads glistening between her fingers like shining silk. Beside her, Yun's jaw dropped.

"What—?"

Mei shook her head and held up a finger, letting him know she'd explain later. They stealthily left the chamber and ran back to the palace kitchen with the box of dreams.

When they were back inside, Yun exclaimed, "You just collected someone's dreams!"

Grinning with anticipation, Mei dug out a large pot from the kitchen cabinets and placed it on the stove. "It's an idea I had," she said as she counted out some grains of rice from the enormous barrel in the corner. Then she splashed some water into the pot, along with the rice. "Remember how good Grandpa's cooking would make everyone feel? So I thought, what *if*..."

"It's a *great* idea," said Yun, who now understood with complete clarity what his sister was about to do.

They waited for the water to boil and the rice to cook. Twenty minutes later, the fragrance of cooked rice filled the kitchen.

"Ready?" Mei grabbed the porcelain box.

"Ready," said Yun, holding the other end of the container.

Together, they tilted the box and poured the dream inside the boiling pot of rice.

Some of the dreamcloud escaped out the sides and evaporated. But something remarkable happened with the clouds that did make it inside the pot. There was a sparkle of glowing yellow showers, like mini fireworks. The sparkles sank into the cooked rice and dissolved. A moment later, the rice looked as it normally did, but smelled more fragrant than any rice Mei and Yun had ever cooked.

"It's like the chef said," said Yun. "Anything can be made into a delectable dish."

"Let's try it first, to see if it's actually delectable." Mei's palms were sweaty, and her skin tingled with excitement.

On the count of three, each sibling ate a spoonful of rice.

Warmth bubbled up their bodies, filling them with elation and airy happiness. They suddenly felt like leaping into the air and doing somersaults around the kitchen. They wanted to skip and dance and shout at the top of their lungs until the whole city woke up.

They didn't do any of that, of course. All they did was stand rock still and look at each other.

"*Whoa*," whispered Yun.

Mei nodded. "Grandpa's secret ingredient."

✳

Now that they'd tested their very first dream, the twins needed more. Lots more. They needed to test the dreams in batches and know exactly which ones were good and which ones were bad, the same way one tests spices and ripe vegetables. Experimentation, they'd decided, was the logical next step if they were to understand these wisps of dreams and what they signified.

Once more, the twins stepped outside into the night. "We can't stop at each and every window," said Mei, looking at the dark buildings. "It'll take too long."

"Plus people will become suspicious," added Yun.

They thought about what to do. In the sky above, clouds drifted one by one across the shining moon.

"Wait a minute," said Yun. "Isn't that the—?"

Their magic cloud that the Jade Rabbit had granted them was floating above. It hung lower than the other clouds, its delicate puffs grazing the top of the roof.

"Oh, *now* it shows up," groaned Yun with a roll of his eyes. "How ironic."

"Maybe it's attracted to our essence," Mei suggested. "Now that we're quite literally working with dreams."

"You mean, we smell like clouds?" Yun asked.

Mei shrugged, but grinned. "Guess we should add it to our endless list of questions for the Jade Rabbit, if we ever actually meet again."

She turned to study the cloud, and then suddenly whirled back toward her brother in excitement. "Yun, what if we collect the dreams from the *sky*?"

"Like on the cloud?" Yun blinked. "Well, it's not the craziest thing we'd have done in the last twenty-four hours. It'll be much faster, that's for sure. Just one question though: how would we collect the dreams from up there?"

Mei thought for a few moments. "Hmm. When I got the princess's dreams into that box, I could almost *feel* them in my hands. Maybe we can reel them in, like fishing!"

Yun's eyes brightened. "I know where they keep the fishing poles in the kitchen."

After they gathered the necessary supplies, the twins made their way up the pillar onto the roof again. They climbed onto the soft cloud, which began drifting slowly across the sky.

"There!" Mei pointed to one of the imperial households.

Several of the windows were cracked open; multicolored mists floated from them.

Yun swung the fishing rod over the edge of the cloud they sat on. The fishing rod dangled near the closest window. Strands of the floating purple mist clung onto the hook as Yun reeled it back up. He held the mist in his hands and grinned. "Here's to dreamweaving. Or should I say dreamfishing?"

"Let's stick with the first name," said Mei as she placed the dream into the box. "It sounds catchier."

"Catchier—like catching fish?"

"Stop it with the fishing puns, *please!*"

For the rest of that night, they gathered more dreams until the box was brimming. Some they took from the servants' quarters, some from the royal quarters, even some from a pigeon they'd found sleeping on one of the rooftops. They saw dreams in every color: green like the dewy grass in the morning; purple-tinged dreamclouds, the color a deep shade of lilac; sunshine yellow; hues of blue, from the pale blue of the sky to the deep blue of the Pearl River in summertime. They also gathered strands of black dreams. As the night went on, black and green dreams began to outnumber the others by far.

"There's a meaning behind the colors," said Yun as he examined the box. "Remember, the Jade Rabbit said nightmares are bright green and black, which stand for anger and fear."

"Like the night of the Mid-Autumn Festival," agreed Mei, remembering how they saw bright green smoke from the neighbors' windows. "Why would Grandpa add those to the mooncakes?"

Yun wrinkled his forehead in thought. "I know when I have nightmares, they take over until I wake up in a panic."

Again, Yun had made an astute observation. It is peculiar, the amount of power a nightmare has: it tends to distort all previous dreams, and has the unique ability to scare a sleeping individual awake. Even if you have the best dream ever, one where you're flying through the infinite skies over lush green meadows, if a nightmare crawls in, it would hurl you toward the earth at eighty miles an hour until you wake up in a cold sweat. Meanwhile, the opposite never happens—no good dream ever seems to follow a nightmare, and no one has ever been woken up because a dream was too good to be true.

Yun closed his eyes. "That's what happened: the original dreams in the jar were good ones, but they got tainted by a nightmare. They *changed* over time."

They thought back to the days leading up to the festival. The rolling clouds, the moody villagers. The spinning events that followed after Grandpa was taken. No doubt, some part had drenched the dreams in the jar, distorting them into nightmares. All by-products of Lotus's curse.

"Most of the purple dreamclouds came from the servant's quarters," continued Yun. "Perhaps they stand for dreams of status and work. I'm not sure about blue...I remember seeing blue clouds above Smelly Tail often."

"Maybe earthly, peaceful pleasures?" suggested Mei.

"Maybe. We'll need to test them all, that's for sure. And that means we might need help from Chef Fan." Yun yawned. "We can do it first thing in the morning. Sorry, but I'm exhausted. You'd think a perk of being a dreamweaver is to never get tired."

"If only," agreed Mei. "It feels like it's been forever since we slept peacefully."

The twins put away their fishing rod and porcelain box, then lay down on the soft cloud. It was the perfect bed—safely above the rest of the city, away from harm. As they were slowly drifting to sleep, they thought of Lotus again. Lotus, who had trapped the people of the City of Ashes inside a fog—a nightmare fog. *A dreamlike state*, the Jade Rabbit had said.

Mei murmured, "No wonder the Jade Rabbit took Lotus's baby. It was for her son's own safety."

"Yes, I'm sure the Jade Rabbit regrets granting Lotus her powers," said Yun sleepily. "I understand why she did what she did, though. The Noble General sounds like the biggest jerk to walk the land." He gave a wide yawn. "It's interesting. The powers the Rabbit gave her almost remind me of our own dreamweaving abilities. Not exactly, of course, but similar in essence. I wonder if they came from the same source."

"Well, we didn't get our abilities from the Jade Rabbit," said Mei. "Ours was passed down in the family."

"It had to start somewhere though, right?" said Yun. "We know it'd be on Mama's side, because of her and Grandpa—" He stopped. "Well, we never knew Grandpa's birth parents, but he didn't either. Grandpa was adopted, remember? He said he doesn't know who his birth parents were, and—"

Yun suddenly sat up.

"His birth parents," Mei repeated, who looked as startled as Yun. "He was adopted in our village when he was still a baby. You don't think...?"

"It all happened seventy years ago. The timeline fits. Grandpa must be the baby in the story. Which means that Lotus... *Lotus* was his mother."

Mei nodded weakly. "Which means Lotus is *our* great-grandmother."

There was a long silence as the twins processed this shocking discovery. Then Yun grinned.

"If Fu-Fu thinks the Noble General's bad, wait till he hears about *our* ancestor."

CHAPTER TWENTY-THREE

二十三

Dream Dumplings

When morning arrived, Mei and Yun went to find Chef Fan to make a deal. The chef was in a crankier mood than usual, as was everyone else at the palace.

"They're saying two intruders were found in the Imperial Library," the chef said as he bludgeoned a large eggplant. "I don't know what kind of dangerous, cunning criminals they must be, to be able to break into such a secure place. Be on high alert, you hear?"

"Oh, yes, of course, Chef Fan," Yun said, wiping eggplant from his cheek. "We would tell you right away if there's something amiss."

"Fine, fine. Now what's all this—who's this girl?" Chef Fan demanded, turning to face Mei.

"My sister," said Yun. "She's thinking about joining the

kitchen staff. I'd like to teach her some basics, if you could give us a place to work—"

"*What?*" Chef Fan roared. "I don't have time for you to waste on—OW!" The twins watched with interest as the chef tried to subdue Bendan, who'd emerged from under the chef's hat and begun pecking at his ear.

"We could watch your bird while we work, of course," offered Mei.

Chef Fan brightened at the suggestion. Five minutes later, the twins found themselves, along with Bendan, installed in a small, empty room with a tiny stove where they could practice cooking.

"You take good care of that bird, you hear?" said the chef as he was leaving.

"Don't worry," Yun reassured him. "Mei practically lived with the birds in the trees back home."

Throughout the day, the twins tested batches of dreams. Tasting blue-colored dreams brought calm thoughts—the lighter the shade of blue, the calmer the thought. No problem seemed too big, no hurdle unbeatable. Getting the stolen pages back from Fu-Fu and lifting a seventy-year-old curse? Easy as rice balls.

Purple-shaded dreams brought mixed feelings of ambition and discontentment. After a sip, Mei suddenly wondered if she'd ever be a sword fighter, and was annoyed she had to grow up in a small village where there were nothing but knobby branches. Yun, frustrated with himself for being hopelessly nearsighted and losing at knobby branch duels, vowed to get a pair of eyeglasses once and for all. Madam Hu had been partially right about ambition. It could easily sway over to bitterness. They found they had to pair purple dream-clouds with a dash of yellow or blue, to bring contentment. It was a tricky balance.

Finally, green-tinged dreams were exactly as they'd suspected—terrible-tasting, harsh, sour. Their situation seemed to worsen after one bite—harsh reality set in, like broken shards of glass. How could two puny twelve-year-olds save an entire village, and a cursed city to boot? As if the rest of the room felt the bleakness, chaos broke loose. Bendan nearly escaped from the room, squawking madly. One of the pots boiled over and spilled angry hot water everywhere. The room sweltered with heat from their cooking, and the twins felt liked boiled meat.

"Here, eat this, quick." Yun grabbed a bowl of leftover rice that had blue dreamclouds added.

They each ate and instantly felt better. Mei coaxed Bendan back with some sunflower seeds, and Yun cleaned up the spilled water. When everything was settled, they inspected the dreamclouds they had left. They were surprised to find a large portion had been tainted green by the previous one, like how a single moldy pear taints the entire basket of fruits.

"Once the curse settles here, this will be everyone's permanent mood," said Mei, dumping the rest of the green dreamclouds out so they evaporated into the air.

When Chef Fan came to retrieve the bird a little while later ("That was the most peace I've had in the kitchen in months," he said), they gave him a small spoonful of blue dreamcloud rice and easily convinced him to spend the rest of the afternoon teaching them how to create perfect pork-and-chive dumplings.

Back at the village, dumplings were one of the foods they saved for special occasions, primarily the Lunar New Year. Multiple families would gather to pound the dough and wrap the dumplings together. Mei and Yun remembered trying to mimic their parents' deft wrapping skills when they were little. Somehow, Mama and Baba's dumplings always looked perfect, like satin coin pouches, while the twins' ended up looking like roadkill.

The dumplings symbolize good fortune, their father had told them. *Eat them and you will be rich*.

Mei and Yun were still awaiting their windfall. Perhaps first they needed to make the perfect dumplings.

As they prepared the dumplings, Chef Fan told them what was happening out in the rest of the palace.

"People left and right, babbling like monkeys," the chef said as he pounded the dough. "Nobody can understand them."

"They're just speaking gibberish?" asked Mei.

"No, no, the words aren't *actual* gibberish. But they might as well be, you hear? The imperial physicians are bewildered, like chickens without their heads."

Yun picked up a piece of dough, then scooped a spoonful of filling onto the center. "If all goes well, everyone should be back to normal," he said nervously.

"Let's hope so, kid. Otherwise, things will never be the same again."

※

The twins, disguised in their servant attire, knocked on Princess Zali's door. "Come in," the princess called.

They walked inside accompanied by Chef Fan and two other servants. "Dinnertime, Your Highness," the chef said with a bow. The servants set up the small table in the corner where the princess normally ate, and the chef placed a steaming plate of dumplings in the center. "Today's meal was created with the help of my two special assistants. Greatest pair of assistants I've had, you hear?"

Princess Zali frowned. She shifted her pink dress robe, each layer of the skirt a different shade of rose, and carefully walked over to the table. Her hair was wound in fancy braids through her glistening hair chopsticks. "I hear you," she replied with a raised eyebrow. "This is certainly a surprise."

Recognition slowly registered in her face, and the twins knew she was thinking of last night's encounter in her dream. For several long moments, she simply stared at the dumplings.

"It's part of our plan to convince Fu-Fu," explained Mei.

"The dumplings are part of the plan?"

"You will love it, Your Highness," promised Yun. He hastily added, "Both the dumplings *and* the plan."

Princess Zali glanced at the other servants, who pretended they hadn't been listening to their curious conversation. With a calm composure, she gingerly dipped a dumpling in the vinegar sauce. She took a bite. Mei and Yun held their breaths.

"Hmm." The princess stopped chewing.

"What's wrong?" said Mei with a worried expression.

Her brother sighed. "I knew we shouldn't have added that extra spoonful of soy sauce."

"This is by far..." Princess Zali looked at the twins with an odd expression as they waited anxiously. "...the *best* thing I've eaten all year."

The twins cheered. Then Mei paused and said with a frown, "You're not just saying that to spare our feelings, right?"

"Absolutely not. This is remarkable." Princess Zali swallowed the dumpling, then ate another one. "I'd hire you two as my permanent chefs. No offense and disrespect to the regular kitchen staff, of course," she added to Chef Fan.

"None taken, Your Highness," Chef Fan reassured her.

"Chef Fan helped us a lot," Yun added. "We just added one extra ingredient."

"Speaking of which," said the chef. He turned to Yun and pleaded, "Won't you tell me the secret ingredient? Just a teensy hint?"

"Of course," Yun replied. Ignoring his sister's fervent shakes of the head, he motioned for Chef Fan to lean in. When the excited chef did so, he answered, "It wouldn't BE A SECRET IF WE TELL YOU, WOULD IT?"

Chef Fan rubbed his ear with a wince. "Well played."

"Are you hoping this would amaze Fu-Fu and make him agree to help you?" Princess Zali asked the twins.

"Something like that," Mei said with a cryptic smile. She bounced on the heels of her feet and said, "Do you feel different at all?" Yun nudged her, but she pressed forward. "Any new emotions, new feelings, Your Highness?"

The princess chewed thoughtfully. "As a matter of fact, I do. I feel . . . enlightened. Just earlier I was feeling glum about the whole situation. But every cloud of gloom has a silver lining. You know the bamboo stick Fu-Fu carries all the time?"

"Yes, he's only threatened us with it at least five times," answered Yun.

"I helped him make that. I taught him how to whittle the

point so it's nice and sharp. And these." She reached up and slid one of her sharpened hair chopsticks from her twisted braids. She admired the weaponized end before holding it out to show the twins. "They can stab a grown man to death."

The twins nodded respectfully. Mei had the good sense not to remind the princess that she'd pressed one of those very chopsticks to Mei's neck a few nights before.

"You're a natural at weapon design, Your Highness," said Chef Fan, eyeing the razor-sharp chopstick with a nervous chuckle. "Please do *not* mix those with the imperial kitchen chopsticks, you hear?"

The princess smiled. "Don't worry, I won't. But you're right, I *am* good at making things. Weapons included." She sat up straighter. "I may not ever join my brothers in physical combat. However . . . I can join their ranks through my weaponry. I shall make the empire new weapons—the most effective and surprising weapons you've ever laid eyes on!"

Mei and Yun clapped. And as the princess enjoyed the rest of dinner, they brainstormed ideas for new weapons with her. They were equally astounded and slightly frightened by the princess's whimsical inventions—which included a beaded necklace that poisoned the wearer when it touched the skin and a hidden star-shaped weapon that could kill someone in five different ways, including underwater.

Their spirits rose. Maybe, just maybe, they could reverse the curse on the city, rescue their grandpa and their parents, and turn one bratty nine-year-old into a new friend in the process. The twins only hoped they'd never cross Princess Zali in their future.

After they finished, Mei and Yun exchanged a look.

"Ready for the real test?" asked Mei.

"Better now than never."

✳

Wham! Fu-Fu hit his bamboo stick against the punching bag in his room. *Whoosh! Wham!* The sharp end poked a hole in the bag, and grains of rice toppled out.

The boy was angry at everyone—angrier than he'd ever been before. Angry at those rotten twins, angry at the guards, angry at himself. He hated how nobody took him seriously. How nobody commented on his combat skills. How he'd never be an heir to the throne. How, if word got out that his great-grandfather had been suspected of being a treacherous liar, his namesake would hold even less meaning. He would be no better than a peasant.

Wham! Worst of all, he was stuck with the babbling curse. It struck at odd times of the day. Anything he wanted to say would twist itself into a complex riddle.

The physicians had advised Fu-Fu to lie low in his room until it passed. So there he stayed, in his room of gloom. He gripped the stick and twirled, faster and faster, until momentum sprung it from his fingers across the room. It just missed hitting the servant who chose that moment to walk in.

Fu-Fu glared at him. Normally, he would have snapped, "What do you want?" but given his current speech issues, he remained indignantly silent instead.

"Master Fu-Fu," said the servant with a slightly shaky bow. "The imperial kitchen staff would like to present your dinner."

"Whatever," Fu-Fu grumbled. He threw his stick on his bed.

The servants set up the table. The boisterous chef entered with a hot plate of dumplings and a teakettle. Fu-Fu was taking a drink when two more people walked in the room. He nearly choked on his tea.

"Why—here?" he coughed, pointing at the twins.

"These are my helpers," answered Chef Fan with a bow.

"We just wanted to bring you your food," said the girl with a sweet smile. "We prepared the dumplings ourselves."

Fu-Fu folded his arms tightly to show there was no way he was trying the food, which was no doubt poisoned. The chef seemed to understand.

"I assure you, Master Fu-Fu," said the chef, "this food has not been tampered with, you hear? We imperial chefs take our jobs very seriously!"

"We can take the first bite of whichever dumpling you eat," offered the boy.

Fu-Fu felt words bubbling in his throat. Before he could stop, he pointed at the twins and blurted,

"What tells you what you want to hear,
But hurts you when the truth is clear?"

The siblings glanced at each other. "We're not liars," said the boy. "We're here to help you. The curse has returned."

Fu-Fu was surprised they figured out what he was trying to say. He also desperately wanted to learn more about the curse and all they knew. Unable to communicate such feelings (or perhaps simply refusing to show his interest), he lowered his head and glowered at the dumplings. His stomach rumbled; the food *did* smell amazing. With a scowl, he plucked one of the dumplings with his fingers, sniffed it, and cautiously took a bite.

The rich flavor melted on his tongue. Warmth spread in his stomach. He gritted his teeth together to mask his surprise and joy.

"What do you think?" asked the girl.

Fu-Fu shrugged indifferently. He almost reached for another dumpling, but forced himself to take a slow sip of tea instead.

"We were hoping to talk to you, Fu-Fu," said the boy. "Our names are Yun and Mei. Yun Wu and Mei Wu. You've heard of the Wu clan?"

"Word that means the opposite of yes."

"That's right, neither have we. We don't really have a family namesake. At least, we thought we didn't."

"Today we found out we're related to Lotus, a woman who set an ancient curse on an entire city," said Mei.

Fu-Fu eyed the two of them suspiciously. He didn't see where this was going, and his stomach was begging for more dumplings. As nonchalantly as he could, he popped another one into his mouth. "So what?" he said with his mouth full.

"I'm willing to bet a lot of people hate her," said Yun. "They probably hate us, too. Some already do—a woman from that city hit my sister with a cane. Just because we're descendants of Lotus!"

"That's rotten stupid," said the chef with a shake of his head. "What do people expect you to do? Go back in time and reverse the curse?"

"I know!" said Yun. "*We* didn't set the curse, Lotus did."

"Exactly," said Mei. "We are not Lotus. Lotus's actions

are not our own." She glanced at the chef. "Can we have a moment to ourselves? Just me, my brother, and Master Fu-Fu?"

"I suppose," agreed Chef Fan. He and the servants left with perplexed faces, as they weren't quite sure what was going on. The door shut behind them.

Mei and Yun turned back to Fu-Fu. He almost started to grab the bamboo stick, but didn't. For the first time in a long time, he felt calm and willing to listen.

"You might have cousins who like to brag they're descendants of the emperor," said Yun. "But that is silly. The emperor's achievements are not their own. I mean, Lotus was supposed to be a phenomenal poet, but neither Mei nor I can write a limerick to save our lives."

"It's a name, that's all," said Mei. "A very important and distinguished name, sure, but just a name in the end. We're far more valuable than our names alone."

"*You* are valuable," said Yun. There was sincerity in his voice this time. "We control our own destinies, much more than our past does."

Fu-Fu looked down at his bowl.

"Our village is in trouble," Mei continued in a softer voice. "So are our parents. They're trapped in time until the curse is lifted, just as you're trapped speaking in riddles. You can help us, and you can help yourself. Give us the seal to the Imperial Library, so we can prove the Noble General framed Lotus's husband."

"That's the only way we can lift the curse," said Yun.

There was a long silence. Fu-Fu cleared his throat. The words were stuck.

He opened the doors to his sleek oak armoire and dug out Mei and Yun's duffel bags. The twins looked surprised as he tossed them over.

"Thank you," they said.

As the siblings examined the blue-and-white jar Mei had showed everyone onstage during the infamous play, Fu-Fu shuffled to his desk and grabbed a piece of parchment and a writing utensil. He scribbled something on the paper. Avoiding eye contact, he wordlessly handed over the page.

I will get it for you.

The twins stared at the writing. "Are—are you sure?" said Mei.

Fu-Fu nodded. Earlier, he had been in a foul mood, but the colorful dreamclouds' magic that had soaked the dumplings was now settling inside his body the way a feather gently lands on the water. It was a subtle feeling, but a good feeling nonetheless. He didn't know the reason for it, of course, but he now felt that he could handle whatever came his way.

"I'm good at sneaking around," he said. "I—" His mouth contorted, and he finished,

"I have no true weight nor one true size,
Blending with darkness is my disguise.
Here in sun, but not in rain,
Silent, darting, hiding pain."

Fu-Fu pinched his mouth with his fingers. *Stupid babbling curse,* he thought.

The twins looked sympathetic. "You are like a shadow," said Yun wisely. "Excellent riddle."

"Here's a riddle from us," said Mei. She cleared her throat and said, "What must you give in order to keep, and easily breaks without a touch?"

Fu-Fu paused. *Easily breaks? Bones? No, that doesn't make sense. A painted urn?*

Then he got it. "A promise," he managed to say.

"Exactly. We promise we'll break this curse. Together."

CHAPTER TWENTY-FOUR

二十四

The Final Test

Later that evening, the emperor's second son finally returned from his trip to the mountains. Immediately, the officials realized something was wrong.

"Something is wrong with His Majesty's son!" the drivers shouted when they entered the court.

They escorted the prince, who seemed to only speak in babbling riddles, into the palace. They called for the wisest men and women in the palace to decipher the prince's sentences. Altogether, they were able to get a few key words: *storm, weather, tongue, mooncakes.*

They also took the old prisoner accompanying him, the only person who remained calm. By then, the clouds in the sky had started swirling dangerously. On the other side of the Imperial City, Mei and Yun immediately recognized it as the beginnings of what had occurred the night of the Mid-Autumn Festival. As they camped out in the safety of the tiny kitchen where they'd prepared the dream dumplings, a palace messenger arrived.

"I am looking for two twelve-year-old servants," the messenger said hesitantly. "One boy, one girl, almost identical?"

"That's us," said Yun.

"Follow me. You've received an invitation to approach the emperor."

The twins nervously walked across the palace complex with the messenger. They realized they were headed to the large hall where the palace had held the banquet on their first night. When they arrived at the entrance of the hall, the messenger left them with a pair of servants who led them through the enormous doors.

"This way to His Majesty," said one of the servants with a solemn nod.

The twins followed the servants through the great room, then down a long, adjacent corridor, then through another grand hall, until finally they stopped at an imposing doorway. An impressive gold-plated throne the size of a small house stood beyond the open doors. Across the chamber stood someone with their back to them. All Mei and Yun could discern was a tall figure in a fiery red robe.

"...and lock the gates," the person in red was saying to three other servants who stood nearby. Those servants nodded, bowed, then scurried past the newcomers out the door.

The man in red slowly swung around. The pair of servants who had accompanied the twins immediately knelt.

"Good evening, Your Majesty," they said respectfully. Mei and Yun quickly followed suit.

The Emperor of China! Never had they ever thought they'd stand in his presence. His robes looked expensive and trailed behind him like liquid as he walked toward the two kids. He wore a matching red hat and had a long, black beard. "I've been expecting you," the emperor said, giving the twins a curious look. "My daughter Zali told me the strangest tale this morning."

Mei and Yun glanced at each other uncertainly.

"Afterward, she has requested I meet with you two to confirm her story. She says it is of the utmost importance and cannot wait until morning."

"Yes, it's very important, Your Majesty."

The twins took turns explaining the entire story, from the day the emperor's son arrived at their village to when they'd arrived at the Imperial City via a cloud. They explained Lotus's curse on the fabled City of Ashes, and how they'd found evidence that cleared her husband's name. They explained how their grandpa had been wrongly arrested, and how the curse had started to affect people at the palace.

Throughout all this, the emperor listened quietly and did not interrupt. At times his eyebrows rose, and other times he opened his mouth, then closed it without a word. When the twins were done speaking, he didn't speak for a while.

"So, from my understanding," he said quietly, "you've trespassed into my court, disguised yourself as servants, used my wife's seal to sneak into the Imperial Library, and tried to steal a book and a bundle of letters, which you claim are proof against a nobleman who wronged this poet named Lotus?"

"Er, yes," Mei and Yun said.

"May I see the book and letters?"

The twins paused. They had not yet seen or heard back from Fu-Fu since dinner, when they'd given him instructions on where to find the evidence.

"It's in the Imperial Library," said Yun nervously. "You'll be able to find it easily. We'd be happy to show you ourselves."

The room waited for the emperor to speak. It was so quiet that the twins could hear the crickets chirp outside the windows.

"Yes, I knew the Noble General well," he finally said. "He was an advisor to my father. He was not quite himself in his later years. 'The babbling commander,' people called him. Although he was never part of the true royal lineage, a few of his descendants eventually made it in. They were much more pleasant than he was, thankfully." At that, the emperor smiled. "One of them happened to be the mother of my second son, the prince who visited your village. We nobility, you understand, tend to have...complicated family trees. If nothing else, the Noble General was an ambitious fellow, and I credit him for that."

The emperor cleared his throat. "Unfortunately, given your trespassing and blatant disregard of palace rules, as well as your grandfather's *highly* suspicious involvement, I am afraid I cannot take your word at face value. In fact, I find it a most unusual coincidence that the babbling curse came to this place only after you intruders arrived."

Yun's jaw dropped. Mei held her breath.

"My son and his companions have confirmed that the mooncakes given to him by your grandfather were the foulest, most bitter foods they've ever tasted, and that the prince started his babbling mere days after eating one. It seems to me that the three of you—you two and your grandfather—are conspirators in crime."

"But, Your Majesty, we're telling the truth!" insisted Yun. "Your timeline's incorrect. The prince was already affected by the curse when he first came to our village. The mooncakes tasted bad because they were tainted by nightmares, brought about by the curse."

"We told you," added Mei. "We spoke to Lotus, and—"

The emperor held up his palm. "That's enough," he said, his voice firmer. "I'm afraid I have no choice. I'll have one of my guards escort you to the dungeon where your grandfather is staying. The results of the trial will determine your fates, but don't expect it to go well at this rate." He looked up. "Yes, what is it, Fu-Fu?"

Startled, Mei and Yun turned to find Fu-Fu panting in the doorway. The boy had obviously run all the way there. For once, he wasn't carrying his bamboo stick.

Two guardsmen headed toward him. "Wait, Your Majesty," he cried. He patted his pockets frantically. His mouth contorted and he blurted,

"This object has a spine and back,
Yet face and bones are what it lacks,
Inside it all the proof resides,
Alternate messages it does hide."

"Show me," commanded the emperor, halting the guards.

Fu-Fu fumbled inside his pockets and pulled out a wad of letters and a blue book, marked with a piece of silk. He handed them to the emperor, who read through the material and examined the incriminating bookmarked page. Fu-Fu also handed over the glinting empress's seal. Then he stood straight and motioned his hand as if writing. Yun quickly reached into his knapsack and pulled out an old pen and parchment. They waited as Fu-Fu scribbled on the paper and handed it to the emperor.

The emperor read the message out loud. *"'I snuck into the Imperial Library to help the twins. I was the one who let them roam free in the first place, instead of calling the guards on them. Do not punish them, Your Majesty.*

'I know the evidence reflects badly on my great-grandfather's name. But I want Your Majesty to know, I am more than my namesake and my ancestors' actions, however good or bad.

'This is our only hope for ending this curse.'"

Fu-Fu looked pale and scared, but he stood bravely. The twins had never seen him act so mature and wise. It was hard to fathom that less than a week ago, he was the boy who walked around with a permanent scowl on his face threatening to impale people with his stick.

The emperor remained quiet, a calm look on his face. "Very well." He shuffled the letters in his hand. "The way forward is clear, then. I shall command my scholars to release these to the public, and to release a public apology for the wrongful death of Lotus's husband...."

Mei and Yun cheered. Mei threw her arms around Fu-Fu, who blushed deep red but nonetheless seemed pleased. The emperor cleared his throat. Silence fell.

"...if and only if you prove you're—what did you call yourselves? Oh yes. *Dreamweavers*."

"S-Sorry, Your Majesty?" said Yun, not sure if he heard correctly.

"I am afraid the evidence only tells one half of the truth. The other half—that in which you claim to be dreamweavers—remains to be seen. In all my years, I've never once had a chef who claims to use dreams as an ingredient, and I've hired some of the best chefs in the country."

Mei and Yun exchanged a look. "You want us to demonstrate our *abilities*?" said Mei.

The emperor nodded gravely. "Make the same mooncakes your grandfather prepared, with dreams as the main ingredient. I expect to eat them and not feel an ounce of unhappiness."

Beside them, Fu-Fu started to protest. The emperor held up his hand, silencing him.

"Be present in the banquet hall in exactly one hour. I will gather the entire royal family and the top officials."

The siblings were so stunned, they didn't quite know how to react. The guards clutched their swords and walked the siblings out.

✳

The emperor's instructions were carried out as quick as lightning. Within thirty minutes, the great banquet hall had been rearranged into a sort of kitchen arena, with a single table that held various bowls and measuring cups. The servants had even procured a makeshift hearth on the side, which the twins could use as a stove.

Seated around the stage were dozens upon dozens of palace officials and royal family members. When Mei and Yun peeked in from the doorway, they nearly froze. This was ten times more nerve-wracking than the act they'd been forced to play on the night of the children's show. Their lives were on the line this time. In fact, hundreds of peoples' lives were at stake if they couldn't lift the curse.

Chef Fan fretfully helped the twins prepare behind the scenes.

"Try not to be nervous, you hear?" he said, his fingers fumbling as he tied the twins' aprons. "A nervous chef makes for weak flavors."

"It's not that much more frightening than Dice of Destiny," said Mei, trying to sound upbeat.

"But we've never made mooncakes before," pointed out Yun, chewing his fingernails. "Much less in front of every prince and princess and high official of China! Plus, I distinctly remember Grandpa saying the mooncakes take *two* days to perfect."

Princess Zali stopped by to wish the twins luck. She sat atop her cushion lifted by her carriers. She looked so regal and imposing that the twins almost sank into their customary bow, until the princess halted them.

"Friends do not bow to each other," she said. Her voice turned quiet. "My father may be hard to please, but if you just do what you did with the dumplings earlier, everything will be all right." She looked down the hall behind them. "In fact, my latest request has just been fulfilled. I will take my leave. Good luck, Mei. Good luck, Yun."

As the princess was carried back to join the rest of the royal spectators, there was a scuffle behind them. A servant ran up to the group, panting. "Mei and Yun Wu?" he said to the twins.

The siblings nodded.

"The princess's earlier request has been granted. Your guardian will be joining us for the spectacle."

Mei and Yun exchanged an incredulous look. The servant motioned down the hallway. Walking down the corridor was a group of guards. In the center of them was . . .

"Grandpa!" shrieked the twins.

His beard had grown longer, unshaved on the journey to the Imperial City, and he seemed thinner and slightly worn. His feet and hands were chained, the same way Mei and Yun's had been in the dungeon. But it was him. He blinked at the twins. His surprise then gave way to relief.

"Am I right to think you arrived earlier than we did?" he said in amusement. "I'll have to tell the emperor's son about cloud travel next time. His food wouldn't have gotten as stale as it did during the long carriage ride."

After a lot of hugs, the twins started to tell Grandpa about everything that had happened. They wanted to tell him about the Jade Rabbit, about dreamweaving, about the curse. But Grandpa gently stopped them in the middle of their first sentence.

"I understand the emperor has put you two to the test," he said. "I will share with you a quick-and-easy recipe for mooncakes." With that, he quickly rattled off the steps as Yun fervently scribbled the notes on a piece of paper.

"Will they be just as good as yours?" asked Mei.

"Yes, they will taste just as good as mine," Grandpa reassured them. "It's still my recipe; it's just the one I use when I'm in a hurry. That part is simple. The challenge is making them even better, so much that they bring the eater pure happiness."

"We know how to do that. We found your jar of—you know."

"The problem is, most of it's empty now," added Yun anxiously.

Earlier, the twins had tried to gather as many dreamclouds as they could. But the beginnings of the curse had cast the Imperial City in a gloom similar to their village's, and the few dreams they could gather from sleeping people had been as turbulent as the sky above. They only had a few glistening strands to work with.

"No, my dears," said Grandpa urgently. "There's more to it. Had I known the mooncakes that day were tainted by nightmares, I would have done something different at the last minute."

"Done what?"

"You see, there is a way to combat the nightmares, all its anger and worries. Think about it. All nightmares stem from one thing: fear. Nightmares are when the person's imagined worst-case scenarios present themselves as bigger than life. But a little bit of patience, and—"

A gong echoed from the room. "Five minutes to start!" someone inside shouted. "Take your seats!"

"Patience and . . . ?" asked Yun.

"And what? What else?" pressed Mei.

But the guards got between them and pushed Grandpa along before he could finish.

"He probably meant patience plus jokes," piped up Chef Fan, who had been not-so-secretly listening to their whole conversation. "Cooking is an art, and as with all artists, there's always going to be someone who dislikes your creation. Some spoiled brat who hates fish, for instance, or an adult who refuses to eat spinach. But you just laugh them off." He clapped his large hands on the twins' shoulders. "I have to go join the audience. Smack all those unwelcome thoughts out of your heads, you hear?"

The chef left Mei and Yun alone in the hallway. They looked dazed.

"Okay, for some reason, I don't think Grandpa was going to say 'jokes,'" said Yun, talking quickly. "We need something that counters the fear. Think. What is the opposite of fear?"

Mei thought. "Bravery. Courage."

"That'll be hard. I've never been particularly brave."

"That's not true," said Mei, frowning at her brother. "Why would you say that?"

"*You're* the brave one. Everyone knows that." Yun was embarrassed to admit this and lowered his head. "I'm the cautious one. I wish I was never afraid of things, like you."

A week ago, Mei might have agreed with her brother. But now she pointed out, "Being brash and being cautious are not the same as bravery and fear. You think I wasn't afraid when we were in the City of Ashes, or in the Temple of Fire, or when we got separated at the palace? You thought I wasn't scared during Dice of Destiny?"

She thought of Princess Zali's words to her days ago, and added, "You could've chosen not to come on this adventure, but you did, in spite of your fear. Not once did you think of *not* doing this."

Yun had never thought of it that way. "Courage and fear," he murmured. "They're like two sides of the same coin, aren't they?"

Mei nodded slowly. "You can't find courage unless you have a certain amount of fear."

Yun's eyes lit up. "I think I figured out what Grandpa wants us to do."

The gong sounded again. A servant poked his head out the back door. *In your places!* he mouthed.

"Ready?" Mei asked.

"Ready," Yun replied.

✳

They entered the banquet hall together. The hundreds of eyes and deafening silence that surrounded the stage made them nearly stumble. The emperor sat in the center, his face impassive. The empress sat next to him, frowning slightly as she cupped her hand protectively around the glistening phoenix seal at her waist. (No doubt she did not like seeing the thieves who'd broken into her quarters.) The twins quickly took their places at the table as a guard announced the rules. They realized with a jolt that it was the same guard who had presided over the Dice of Destiny game.

"As per the emperor's request, the pair of prisoners before you will prepare special mooncakes," he announced. "They will be using their unique abilities—dreamweaving, they call it. The emperor will taste the final mooncake. If it is deemed satisfactory, then they will be released."

The audience nodded and murmured amongst themselves.

"You will have two hours," the guard told the twins. "Beginning . . . *now*."

If you've never cooked in front of hundreds of people, it may be hard to imagine the pressure Mei and Yun felt in that moment. First, imagine a room full of the strictest, hardest-to-please people (your schoolteacher from two years ago, a supervisor at the local supermarket, or the crabby neighbor from down the street). Imagine hundreds of them, sitting side by side and frowning as you stood before them. Imagine them muttering disapprovingly each time you lifted your hand or moved an inch.

The table had been filled with various ingredients provided by the chefs. The audience watched as Mei and Yun spread black sesame seeds in a large skillet. The sesame seeds sizzled, and a strong nutty aroma filled the room, making some audience members' mouths water.

They watched as Mei mixed sugar and flour in a bowl. They oohed when Yun rolled the sticky dough into a perfect ball. ("I taught him a lot; he's grown so fast, you hear?" Chef Fan could be heard weeping in the audience).

The twins' grandfather watched from the sideline with a determined look. At a glance, he did not seem at all worried, but if one watched him carefully, they could see his feet fidgeting slightly in their chains, and whenever he swallowed, the lump in his throat trembled.

The audience looked on in puzzlement as the twins took a decorative porcelain jar and seemed to remove invisible things with their hands. ("It's just like that play we saw," one of the kids whispered.) The siblings smeared the invisible strands into the mooncakes' filling.

As the mooncakes baked, the banquet hall brimmed with its sweet aroma. Stomachs grumbled, and several audience members flagged down the servants and requested a late-night snack from the kitchen.

Down in the center of the room, Mei and Yun wiped their sweaty foreheads—partly from the heat, partly from nerves. Finally, the mooncakes finished baking. They carefully removed the golden little cakes.

"Now for the final touch," Mei murmured to Yun. "Care to do the honors?"

"We'll do this together."

The twins closed their eyes and took a deep breath. They thought of their fears at that moment—how the babbling curse might stay if they failed to please the emperor with their mooncakes, how Grandpa might lose the trial. They then delved into another, deeper layer of more profound fears—how they might never see their parents again, how they might end up alone in the world. And it was a terribly frightening world at times. The riddling curse and the City of Ashes aside, the world also carried with it the unknown. The unknown, the twins sensed, was perhaps the most unsettling thing of all.

But that didn't mean they couldn't be courageous when facing it—or any of these fears.

They leaned in close to the mooncakes and breathed out at the same time. With that breath, they imparted this secret knowledge they shared, this tiny bite of wisdom, into the mooncakes. Although the audience couldn't detect it, the steam that rolled off the mooncakes glowed ever so slightly—pure white, then black, then back to the regular steam that one might find wafting over a bowl of hot soup.

"They're ready, Your Majesty," Yun said. He and Mei placed the gleaming mooncakes on the table and bowed.

One of the servants quickly gathered the plate and carried

it to the emperor. The room was silent as the servant sampled a cake for signs of poison. His eyebrows raised, and he gave a quick nod to indicate everything was okay.

The emperor carefully cut into one of the crumbly mooncakes and chewed.

He raised his head and looked at the twins, then back at the mooncakes.

"Your Majesty?" someone piped up nervously.

"What do you think, Father?" called Princess Zali.

There was a long pause. A small smile spread across the emperor's face. "Impressive," he finally said softly. He peered at the twins and gave an approving nod. "You have demonstrated your skills."

As soon as he'd finished, cheers erupted from the back of the room. It was Fu-Fu and Princess Zali. They turned to each other and hugged one another. Their excitement slowly spread to the rest of the audience, who either clapped respectfully or else whistled and yelled like it was the Lunar New Year's celebrations.

"I want to try some, too, Your Majesty!" someone else called. Others echoed in agreement. There was then a long line as all the royal members and officials of the Imperial Palace waited to try a bite of the twins' mooncakes.

Mei and Yun went to the side of the room to join Grandpa. The three of them were overwhelmed, and for several moments, none of them could say anything. Grandpa wore a proud smile, and tears welled in his eyes. He started to say something, when a squawk interrupted the room.

"*Squawk! Thank you! Thank you!*" Bendan poked his head out of Chef Fan's pocket and flew off in a burst of bright feathers. He knocked over an urn, clawed the drapes on the windows, and nearly flew into one of the princess's large hairdos, thinking he'd found a new nest. The chef yelped for the mischievous parrot to come back, with threats that he'd cook the parrot for breakfast.

"Wait!" Mei reached into her pocket and stepped forward with an outstretched palm. In her hand was a pile of sunflower seeds.

The parrot turned, spotted the delicious morsels, and practically dove onto her palm. Mei patted the parrot's head gently, cooing, "There, there," and Bendan began helping himself to the seeds without uttering a peep.

Chef Fan's eyes lit up. "Sunflower seeds," he murmured. "That's it! Sunflower seeds, you hear?" He approached the bird, who fluttered back into the air. The chef picked up one of the seeds and held it up. Bendan flew toward it immediately and rubbed his head against the chef's wrist, making a purring noise that reminded the twins of Smelly Tail.

"Looks like you've finally solved your bird problem, Chef Fan," sighed one of the servants as he carefully placed the urn back upright.

"Yes. Who knew the answer was so simple?"

A loud snort came from behind them. They turned to the emperor, who was watching the mess while trying not to smile. "You mean after all this time, Chef Fan, you never once thought to tame the bird with *food*?"

The chef burst into loud chuckles, until he bent over from laughing so hard. The servants started to laugh, too, then the royal members and the officials. Finally, Mei and Yun joined in.

CHAPTER TWENTY-FIVE

二十五

Reunion

The successful mooncakes had given the palace the extra dosage of encouragement they needed in the light of the impending curse. Afterward, when the others had all gone to bed, Mei and Yun stayed up in the guest room the emperor had offered Grandpa and the twins. Finally, they were able to tell him the whole story: about meeting the Jade Rabbit and Lotus, about their dreamweaving adventures, about trying to end the curse.

After the twins had recounted their adventures, Grandpa lowered his head. "As I'm sure you know, I owe you two an apology," he said. "I'm sorry I did not reveal the truth about your parents earlier. Or the dreams, which I know you've been seeing your whole lives. I wanted to protect you, but I realize now that I was foolish in doing so."

"We understand," said Yun. "It's all right. If all goes well, we should see them again. The question is how."

Although the emperor offered them full permission to stay at the palace complex while they waited for Grandpa's trial (he'd strongly hinted that Grandpa would go free, that the trial was merely a formality at this point), Grandpa had advised the twins to leave the palace and return to the City of Ashes to see Lotus right away. But even the emperor's fastest horses could not make it there in less than a week.

"Perhaps we can speak to her in our dreams," Yun suggested, but Grandpa shook his head.

"From what you've told me, I'm afraid Lotus's case is particularly unique," he said. "You must be physically present in her dream chamber to speak with her. She is a relic in time, after all."

Mei looked out the window at the sky. Lightning streaked against the dark night. The magical cloud that had transported them had vanished into the sky's swirling storm.

"Now's a great time for the Jade Rabbit to help us," she sighed.

"The Jade Rabbit hasn't talked to us since that first day in the City of Ashes!" said Yun. "Don't get me wrong, it did help transport us here, which we're grateful for. But I'm beginning to wonder whether it's sitting back watching us in amusement."

"Yun, dear Yun," said Grandpa with a slight shake of his head. "Think of the number of people in the Imperial City alone. Now think of all the people in the other cities and villages across China. You are not the center of the Jade Rabbit's world."

He rearranged the blankets around his feet. "That said, I am familiar with the Jade Rabbit. More than most, I'd say."

The twins exchanged a triumphant look. "We knew it," said Mei. "You're Lotus's son, aren't you?"

Grandpa didn't speak for several long moments. "I figured it out only moments ago, after you told me what had happened," he finally said in a low voice. "It all makes sense now. In the few times the Jade Rabbit and I have crossed paths—always in dreams, mind you—it was always as if the creature was . . . checking on me. It was in dreams that the rabbit reminded me of the gifts I'd been given, and to do good with them. I was never told the specifics of my lineage during these encounters, likely for the same reason I never told you the truth about your own parents. Ignorance, Mei and Yun, is often bliss—but it is the easy way out. Truth is difficult. I am saddened to learn what happened to my parents, and it may take a while for me to process. That said, I've led a good life. It does not define me any more than it defines you.

"Remember, I did not receive my powers from Lotus. Those came after I was born. And my powers—and yours, through your mother—came from the Jade Rabbit itself. I suppose it makes sense the source was the same, and why the powers are similar. Although mine did not have the colossal potential that Lotus's had, they were nonetheless impactful. People often underestimate the power of dreams, of emotions and fears. They're inside us, living alongside the physical world."

"Like yin and yang," finished the twins.

"Precisely."

"So . . ." said Mei after a moment of silence. "If the Jade Rabbit was your, um, de facto guardian, can you summon it?"

Grandpa smiled. "Let me try. First, I must fall asleep."

The twins waited patiently. Soon, their grandpa was snoring lightly, but nothing happened. Just as Mei started to grow fidgety and Yun started to grow bored, a pool of moonlight filled the center of the kitchen. Moments later, the Jade Rabbit emerged before them.

"Greetings, children," it said. *"I hear from a trusted source your task was successful. Are you up for one last trip?"*

※

Mei and Yun peeked over the edge of the cloud. Home wasn't far now. They could see the familiar outline of the mountains by their village. Bit by bit, they could see the Pearl River between the hills. They approached the gloom encircling the City of Ashes. As their own cloud drifted into the mist, the moon slowly faded from view and disappeared from the sky. It had been ten days since their departure from their village. The curse was still in place.

The cloud floated above the Temple of Fire, near the top of the stairs. Mei and Yun jumped off with their belongings. The ghostly hooded figures were still there, standing in the same spots they'd been days ago, as if time wasn't a concern. It likely wasn't to them.

The twins entered the temple and made their way up to the second landing where Lotus's dream chamber was. The single dancing flame flickered in the dark room. They walked toward the pillows and laid their heads on them. Moments later, they were asleep.

Sunlight flooded the chamber. Mei and Yun found themselves standing before Lotus.

"You've returned," Lotus said calmly. "I've been waiting."

"We did it." Mei dug into her bag and took out a scroll. "What is this?"

"It's a decree from the emperor," said Yun. He read,

> *"Gardener Wong of the defunct City of Blossoms was wrongly accused of treason. He was framed by one of the members of our rank, the Noble General. Effective immediately, his name will be cleared of all crimes, and the public shall remember him as the kind gardener who brought beauty to this world.*
>
> *In addition, the palace has made public once again its impressive collection of poems, in honor of Gardener Wong's wife, Lotus, distinguished poet of the City of Blossoms.*
>
> *Signed,*
> *The Emperor of China"*

Stamped beneath was the dragon seal of the emperor. Lotus took the scroll and read it again silently. Then again. She couldn't seem to believe it.

"How?" she finally said in a hoarse voice.

Once again, the twins explained the entirety of their adventures in the Imperial City. "It wasn't easy," admitted Mei. "But we had lots of help."

"One of the kids who helped us was the great-grandson of the Noble General," Yun mentioned.

Lotus blinked. "Interesting. Why did he decide to help you?"

Yun shrugged. "The palace children are not that different from us, really."

"Now for your end of the deal," said Mei. "Lift the curse."

Lotus's hands tightened against the scroll so that her knuckles turned white. The scroll trembled. "I don't know if I can," she murmured.

"What do you mean?" asked Yun. "Certainly you can lift the curse."

"I don't know if I can," Lotus said again. "Not after all these years. It's easier to remain as I am, as the vengeful poet who burned down an entire city with her words." She lowered her head. "It's easier to do that, rather than admit I was a fool bent on revenge. In that sense, I fear the Noble General bested me in the end."

Yun opened his mouth to protest, but Mei elbowed him. They waited as Lotus walked across the chamber to study the painting with the blossom trees.

"I had a choice," Lotus said softly with her back to them. "There's an old proverb: *endure one moment of anger, and escape a hundred days of sorrow.* I could have chosen a peaceful life for me and my son. I'll never know what became of him."

"But he's alive!" interrupted Yun.

Lotus stiffened. She faced them and said, "What did you say?"

"Your son is alive," joined in Mei. "He's... he's our grandpa."

It was not the kind of first meeting one usually has with their great-grandmother. Lotus stared at the twins with a mixture of shock and anger. She studied their faces more, looked closely until she recognized her own features in them. Slowly, her surprise melted into relief and sadness.

"You're telling the truth," she whispered.

"We should have revealed that earlier," Yun said sheepishly. "We figured out we were related when we were in the Imperial City."

"Where is my boy now?" Lotus asked urgently. "How is he? Has he lived a good life?"

"Yes, Grandpa has always been cheerful," said Mei. "Even when life gets hard, he sees the silver lining. Like when Grandma passed away, he says he still sees her in his dreams."

Tears welled in Lotus's eyes and trickled down her cheek. "And what about his own children?"

"Our mother," answered Yun quietly. "She is your granddaughter."

"You told me your parents came here. Are they still in the city?"

The twins nodded. "Along with many other families," added Mei.

Lotus seemed to be rendered speechless. She then clasped her hands and turned to the painted scrolls on the wall. "A human flows downstream and remains dust forever," she whispered.

Then she said with the trace of a smile,

"Yet from the dust rises
New life, the seedling of a flower,
And it blooms lovingly until
The entire field shines with its splendor."

The poet no longer looked upset or angry, but calm. Peaceful.

A sudden gust of wind shook the walls. "What is happening?" said Lotus, bewildered.

The shaking extinguished the light in the chamber, plunging everything into darkness. Mei and Yun grabbed each other's hand. They both opened their eyes wide but couldn't see a thing. Everything around them was pitch black. For a moment, the twins wondered if they'd lost their vision.

Then wisps of colored dreamclouds sprung up here and there, sparkling threads within the mists bursting in yellows, purples, blues. Like fireworks, only there was not a peep. The twins huddled together, their eyes fixed on the bright colors that surrounded them.

The chamber returned to its original state. The paintings were slashed, the gildings tarnished. The only thing different was that the flame in the corner was gone.

Mei and Yun glanced wordlessly at each other, then raced back downstairs and out into the moonlight.

The city buildings were still as desolate as before, broken and partially ruined. Only now, the streets were filled with people. Real, solid people. Men and women and children walked down them, calling to one another, laughing, chatting.

A shimmering white light appeared before them. For the first time, the Jade Rabbit bowed before them.

"Thank you, children. I think it is time for you to go home."

✳

For almost a year after, villages and towns across China gossiped about a series of unusual incidents that had been happening across the country. Long-lost family members and friends suddenly reappeared, some who had been gone as many as fifty years, apparently showing no signs of aging. These people were utterly surprised at the others' claims that they'd disappeared for years on end, and insisted they were surely mistaken. There were also reports about a cursed city being restored deep in the mountains, and how several prominent officials, including a prince, babbled in riddles for three days before being inexplicably cured. Whether these stories were pure fantasy or real, no one but those who knew the truth could say.

Around the same time, the unusual weather hovering over a small village beside the Pearl River returned to normal. That was the day Mei and Yun returned. They were greeted by frantic hugs and shouts of concern. Madam Hu whipped up a bowl of her famous soup dumplings to warm the twins up.

Madam Hu then led the village in an effort to appeal for Grandpa's release.

"We acted terribly," she said to the nodding villagers. "Old Wu has always been there for us, through thick and thin. Why, it's simply nonsensical that he should be arrested!"

Unfortunately, as all the farm animals had died from the sudden snowstorm, there was nothing fast enough to deliver the appeal to the emperor. Fortunately, Elder Liu revealed he'd been keeping a flock of carrier pigeons he'd kept warm and well fed in the back room of his house. Despite the twins' protests that it really wasn't necessary, he volunteered his best and strongest pigeon, which managed to fly to the Imperial City in record time. It flew back with a note from the emperor pardoning Grandpa. It also brought two small wrapped gifts—one for Mei, one for Yun—both signed

From the Princess of Weaponry. Inside Mei's package was a tiny ceremonial dagger; the familiar decorations on the handle reminded her of the princess's deadly chopsticks. Inside Yun's was a pair of eyeglasses.

Two weeks later, Grandpa returned. The entire village celebrated with an enormous feast that rivaled the Mid-Autumn Festival. Every villager pitched in with leftovers and extra food they'd scraped from their homes. The festivities lasted well into the night.

"Grandpa, there's something we need to tell you," Mei said when they headed home.

"What is it, dear Mei and Yun? It's not about poor Smelly Tail, is it?"

"No, no, Smelly Tail is fine," said Yun. Indeed, the cat had been well and healthy when the twins returned from their journey. It seemed the cold weather had shooed an unusually large number of rats inside the house, which offered a steady food supply for the hungry cat.

"It's just that a lot of things have happened," said Mei. "But there's one that hasn't . . ." She struggled to hide her disappointment. Next to her, Yun looked away.

"Mm-hmm," said Grandpa wisely. "Your parents have not returned."

After Lotus had restored the city, the first thing the twins had wanted to do was search the streets for their parents. But they quickly realized it wasn't that simple. Undoing the seventy-year-old curse apparently took a while. Those who had been there earliest were the first to emerge from their dreamlike state. The twins' parents were still frozen in line. It was like peeling an onion, layer by layer. The Jade Rabbit told them there was no way of knowing how long it might take.

"We've reversed the curse," said Yun, adjusting his new glasses. "We've waited. Everyone should be free now."

"These things take time," Grandpa said gently. "Tell you what. Why don't the three of us take a trip to the city tomorrow?"

The twins hadn't been back since their last encounter with Lotus. They'd hoped to see her again, but the Jade Rabbit had informed them that now that Lotus had found peace, she would no longer be in the dream world or the physical world. (*"There is a realm beyond these worlds, where even I have no knowledge of,"* the magical creature had said.) They'd kept their ears peeled for news from the city. The only notable thing that happened was a week ago, when three young travelers appeared at their village, and the ancient Elder Liu stated in shock that he recognized them. It turned out the three friends had been traveling to the village to visit the old man fifty years ago, and had stayed for what they thought would be one night at the City of Ashes but was actually half a century.

The twins heard nothing about their parents.

"Pack your bags tonight," Grandpa insisted. "We'll go first thing tomorrow."

Uneasiness curled in the twins' stomachs. They reluctantly agreed, and went inside to prepare their bags.

But it turned out they didn't need to. Early the next morning, as the sun barely peeked over the mountains, there came a knock at the door. Grandpa went to answer it. He came back a moment later and poked his head in the twins' bedroom. His face was unreadable.

"Mei, Yun, there are people here to see you."

The twins exchanged a look. They slowly went to the door. Their hearts leapt.

Their mother and father stood on the porch, appearing exactly as they'd looked six years ago.

CHAPTER TWENTY-SIX

二十六

The Dream Fishers

None of the villagers were awake by the time a mysterious figure emerged on one of the clouds drifting above. Nor did anyone see the two smaller figures following close behind with straw baskets and porcelain jars. They sat cross-legged on the cloud, watching as the fisherman reeled in his catches and placed them carefully inside the jar. The moon illuminated these individuals, a girl and a boy.

"Hurry, Grandpa," the girl said. "We must get ready for the festival tomorrow."

"Yes, Mei's boyfriend is coming—I wonder if he'll bring his bamboo stick," teased the boy.

The girl whacked him, nearly knocking his glasses off.

"Kidding, just kidding," he hurried to say. "What I really do wonder is whether the princess will bring her latest invention.

It sounds a bit like a catapult, but fits in the palm of your hand. I read about it in her last letter, and it made my whole body shiver."

"Whatever they bring, we'll have to make the best mooncakes ever," said the girl.

The fisherman reeled in his rod. More glittery threads clung to the bottom of the hook, golden yellow and blue as the ocean. He gently swept the threads into a jar. "They will be good, don't worry," the old man remarked with a smile. "Nothing but the best for our special guests from the Imperial City."

Down below, a man and a woman waited for the trio's return. They bore an uncanny resemblance to the boy and girl. The man sat beside the Pearl River, reading scrolls under the moon. The woman hummed quietly to herself amidst a fog of blue; a butterfly clip glinted in her hair.

The moon that night was nearly a perfect orb. The shadow of the Jade Rabbit winked in the sky.

❊

Author's Note

The idea for *The Dreamweavers* came to me in the form of a half-conceived image. I was thinking of the clouds that drift beneath the moon on a starry night, when I pictured a fisherman sitting on top of them. Suddenly I thought, *What if there was a fisherman who cast his line from the clouds?* And instead of fishing for *fish,* he was fishing for peoples' dreams? One question led to another, and this book is the result of my search for those answers.

My first book, *No Ordinary Thing,* was an ode to American history. *The Dreamweavers* is a letter to my Chinese roots. It's important to keep in mind that *The Dreamweavers* is, above all else, a fantasy. While some parts of the book are drawn from historical fact, and while I conducted research before and during the writing process, I am by no means an expert on Chinese history. The purpose of this book is not to instruct, but to transport you to a magical new world!

That said, here are a few more details about some of the historical, cultural, and mathematical elements of the story that you might be interested in learning more about.

On Chinese Mythology

While writing *The Dreamweavers,* I drew elements from childhood stories, including oral tales passed down to me from my grandparents. Back when I lived in Beijing, the Monkey King was one of my favorite characters, and I watched the TV show fanatically as a delighted four-year-old. It wasn't until I'd finished the first draft of this book that I actually ordered a translated copy of *Journey to the West* (an enormously thick text, and that was just the first volume). In this incredible adventure novel, I learned that it was common in ancient Chinese stories for the characters to switch between the physical world and the dream world. This theme wove itself prominently into *The Dreamweavers.*

There are many variations of the origin of the Jade Rabbit, who is a very popular character in Chinese culture. The version most familiar to my parents tells of how the Jade Rabbit is a medicine maker, and you can see its outline on the moon as it pounds herbs into a magical elixir with its mortar and pestle. The tale my grandma learned portrays the creature as a beloved pet to the goddess of the moon, Chang'e. Other variations mention the Jade Rabbit was once a human who transformed into the hare after drinking a forbidden potion. For the purposes of this story, I went with the first legend: a lone rabbit that creates powerful elixirs.

A quick note: the word "jade" often conjures the color

green, and several people have wondered why the Jade Rabbit is not portrayed that way. The reason is that jade actually comes in several naturally occurring colors. While jade jewelry in Europe is bright green like emeralds, for most of China's history, it was often white.

On Chinese Philosophy

The concept of yin and yang comes from Taoism, a Chinese philosophy founded in the 4th century B.C. by the writer Lao Tzu, and is simplified in *The Dreamweavers*. The actual philosophy behind it is far more complicated (involving 64 permutations of hexagrams). Look up the Eight Trigrams if you're feeling courageous, but as my grandma warned, "You can study it for a lifetime and comprehend only half of it."

When the Jade Rabbit mentions to the twins that "a journey of a thousand miles begins with a single step," it was referencing a popular proverb attributed to Lao Tzu.

On Foot Binding

In the story, Princess Zali's feet were bound. For many centuries in China, girls, usually those of the nobility class, had their feet tightly bound with cloth in such a way that their feet were completely reshaped and would not continue to grow. Painful as the binding was, small feet on women were considered a status symbol and a mark of the woman's beauty. Historians believe one of the oldest variants of the popular fairy tale *Cinderella* comes from a short story in the Tang Dynasty, in which one woman's foot fits inside a tiny golden slipper when nobody else's could.

The practice of foot binding, which hampered mobility, was controversial even in its heyday. Many women opposed the practice, and there were emperors who attempted to ban it altogether. Foot binding officially became illegal in the 1900s.

On Homonyms

In the Imperial Library, Mei and Yun discover through a mis-written sign that Lotus's husband had been framed. This is achieved through homonyms—or homophones, specifically. In the Chinese language, there are many words that sound the same out loud, but mean completely different things, the same way the English words *see* and *sea* have different meanings.

On the Mathematics Behind Dice of Destiny

I made up the game of Dice of Destiny that you read about in this story, but the twins' chances of winning are based on actual mathematical principles. You might be wondering, what is the *exact* probability of winning in Dice of Destiny? Turns out the answer requires several calculations. In a nutshell, you would need to figure out the probability of getting a certain score after the first two rolls, then calculate the winning outcomes for the final roll. Keep in mind, once you're too deep in the negatives after two rolls, there's no way of winning. Below is a snapshot of the odds after two rolls (credit for this explanation goes to Jonathan Tannenhauser, Ph.D., mathematician extraordinaire).

SCORE AFTER TWO ROLLS	PROBABILITY OF GETTING THIS SCORE	SUM OF DICE NEEDED ON FINAL ROLL TO WIN THE GAME
20	0.3%	10,8,6,4,-3,-5,-7,-9,-11
18	1.2%	10,8,6,4,-3,-5,-7,-9,-11
16	2.5%	10,8,6,4,-3,-5,-7,-9,-11
14	3.1%	10,8,6,4,-3,-5,-7,-9,-11
12	2.5%	10,8,6,4,-3,-5,-7,-9,-11
10	2.0%	10,8,6,4,-3,-5,-7,-9
8	1.9%	10,8,6,4,-3,-5,-7
7	0.6%	10,8,6,4,-3,-5
6	1.5%	10,8,6,4,-3,-5
5	2.5%	10,8,6,4,-3
4	0.8%	10,8,6,4,-3
3	5.6%	10,8,6,4
1	8.0%	10,8,6,4
0	13.5%	10,8,6,4 (WHERE MEI AND YUN WERE AFTER THEIR SECOND ROLL)
-1	8.0%	10,8,6,4
-3	6.3%	10,8,6,4
-5	4.0%	10,8,6
-6	0.3%	10,8
-7	2.9%	10,8
-8	1.2%	10
-9	1.5%	10

The actual chance of winning the game is 29%. Not *too* grim, but I wouldn't bet my life on it. Would you?

Acknowledgments

This magical book would not be what it is without the wonderful people who helped me weave it into its final stages.

First, a thank you to Christyne Morrell, fantasy author extraordinaire, for reading the story in its earliest draft and providing insights. A huge thank you to my ever-brilliant editor, Kelly Loughman (a.k.a. the Sharp-eye), whose advice and keen mind helped improve the story beautifully. A thank you to the meticulous copyeditor John Simko and the entire team at Holiday House for your support, and Adria Goetz for connecting me with the perfect publisher for my stories. A special thanks to Feifei Ruan, the magnificent cover artist who brought the essence of this story to life.

A big thanks to Jonathan Tannenhauser, my delightful math professor from college, who helped me understand the mechanics behind Dice of Destiny.

A thank you to my family, especially Hayden. Your wonderful wit cheers me up even in nightmares. I wrote and edited much of this book as the dreadful coronavirus pandemic unfolded in 2020, but in spite of the bleakness affecting us all, you were always there beside me.

At its heart, this book is inspired by my own grandparents. Thank you, Grandma and Grandpa, for the stories you shared, and for all you have taught me about Chinese folklore.

Also, a shoutout to Evan, my kid brother, who may or may not have gotten into plenty of mischief like the twins did.

Finally, I strive to bring joy and whimsy to each of my works, but the greatest joy comes from the people who are willing to take a chance on them. Thank you, reader, for being part of this journey.